THE FEMA
BO(

CU00407020

THE FEMALE SADIST
BOOK 2

FETISH WORLD BOOKS

CHAPTER ONE

Now

The scene in that basement. It wasn't nice. It wasn't just the visuals. There was the atmosphere and the dread associated with it as well. It was like a thick thing that hung over the air down there. There were three people down there but there was no talking. No laughing. No interaction at all. Oh maybe there was some interaction. But it came from one person and one person alone. Pippa interacted with the couple that she had disempowered. She had taken the worse that they could offer and then she had set about reaping the worse revenge that she could reap. Except that it wasn't over yet. She hadn't finished yet. She had only just started. Barely started in fact. What she had done to date was merely overpower the two. Let them know that she wasn't playing around. Let them know that they were in dire, dire trouble. And she seemed to be able to do that with ease. The switch. The turn round. The turning of the tables. One minute she was the victim. The next she wasn't and what she did then was proceed to teach Delores and Max a lesson they would never forget. A lesson that would haunt them for the rest of their natural lives. If they survived that is.

Delores, finally thought she must be existing in a nightmare. There had been a time during which she had thought, or accepted that it must be a nightmare. That she would wake up at any time and it would all be over. But that hadn't been when she herself had been the focus of Pippa's attentions. When she had been being worked on by this nut job of a girl, it was like she was in that surreal world from which she would be snatched back into the normal world at any time. But watching Max suffer terribly the way she had, she had been snapped out of her own dream world and into the real world in the worse way possible. Watching Max suffer. Watching him suffer real time. It wasn't fantasy stuff that he had been

subjected to. It wasn't his fantasy or her fantasy that Pippa had subjected him to what she had subjected his balls to the most painful beating and crushing that could be imagined.

"I don't know what the tears are for Delores. You didn't really think you were going to get away with what you two did to me, did you? But, of course you did. Of course you thought I was another of your 'victims'. Course you did. Because this is what you two do isn't it. Respectable in finance circles by day. And by night sick fucks. Except, for some reason neither of you thought there would ever be anyone sicker than you out there. Well you got that wrong didn't you? I think you KNOW now you got that wrong."

Pippa had been speaking as she got Delores down off the stool. It was a little bizarre in that she 'helped' the older woman down. She might have been forgiven for kicking the stool from under her once she had slipped the noose off her head. If she had kicked the stool and let the woman fall to the floor with her hands still behind her. But she hadn't done that. She had gently reversed the bondage that she had applied. She was helping her. But bearing in mind what she had just done to Max, she was helping her, gently helping her down and then into a position that she could cause more hurt and pain. In which she could cause more havoc. The way Pippa worked gently and with skill showed a focus. It showed that this chameleon like woman was working to a target. Like a pre-set trajectory. That she wasn't causing maximum pain and degradation indiscriminately. That she knew what she was doing. And she was doing it in a way that she got the most out of it. Neither Max nor Delores would need to be told that this woman was a sadist of the advanced kind. That much would be obvious. But it would only be obvious on a slowing increasing basis. Like a gentle but a definite ramping up of the pressure on the couple. This was a girl, a woman who knew what she was doing in the most complete

way. Even when she interacted, even when she spoke to either of the two as she worked, she was still working. Using her words as a tool to further their torment. Indeed, the word torment wasn't enough for what she did. Or what she was doing. This couple, Delores and Max, despite what they had suffered so far would have been left with the feeling that their nightmare wasn't over. That there was more to come. And that they didn't know where it was going to end. And that was deliberate. That was what Pippa intended. It was intended that she leave this couple feeling uncertain and afraid for their future.

Pippa kicked a chair in front of where Max was still standing spread legged and bondaged. He was still twisted in that almost sickening way. His psyche trying to protect him from more pain. But in doing so, making him look like a pathetic trapped animal.

"Take a seat Delores. We're going to get acquainted. Intimately acquainted but I need to go make myself more presentable."

Delores sniffed and she sat. There had been just the little spark of something in the back of her mind that was telling her with her hands released and the bondage gone she should fight this woman. At least attempt to get away. Maybe even get help. After all, it was herself and Max who were the victims now. The law was on their side. But the notion was soon dispersed. After seeing what this girl had done to Max, and to herself with very little effort, she would stand no chance in a fight with her. And who knows where that would lead? There was no telling what they would be made to suffer if she tried and failed. That wasn't worth thinking about. But Delores was dumbfounded, shocked that she wasn't then tied again. Or disabled in some way. That she was just allowed to sit on the chair in front of the prosed Max. She sat there but she couldn't believe she was sitting there. It was as though Pippa had instilled her shock – she had done the bit that counted – rendered this couple

7

helpless and useless and now she didn't need to be too cautious. It was like she knew that Delores would be fighting with herself about whether to make a bid for freedom or not. Pippa could smile to herself about those thoughts. She knew that the first phase of her revenge was done and dusted. That it was in the bag. She had gone up into the house, from the basement with that smile across her face. And she had turned the key in the door to the basement with a smile as well. The couple locked in their own basement torture room. Delores weakened but free to move. Max tethered and with wrecked balls. To Pippa it was all about karma. It was all about what went around came around.

"Max, Max can you hear me? Wake up Max we've got to get out of here."

Delores wasn't sure if Max could hear her or not. He had been moaning and rolling his head from side to side. He was conscious. Or semi-conscious at the very least. Delores was impatient but she understood. She was sickened by what Pippa had done to him. She had been shocked what the girl had done to her.

"Forget it Delores. We're fucked. Can't you see that?"

He was awake, sort of. But he spoke as though he had been drugged. The only drug that had been administered to Max was pain. And he had been overdosed on that. Delores looked up at him from her chair. She knew what he was saying was the truth. She didn't want to accept that but knew that she had no choice. This was the conversation or the state of mind that Pippa knew would be taking place as she went to Delores's walk in dressing room come closet to choose an outfit.

"Unless of course in your plans, when you designed this place, you built in an escape. In case you thought this day would ever come when some fruit loop would turn the tables on us and trap us in our own dungeon. I mean you're clever Delores. Surely you thought about

8

that, right?"

Max was being ironic. But it was clear that the predicament had, or was turning the couple against each other. Pippa would know that as well. She would know what was happening down there right now. As she applied the pale foundation to her face and then started on her lips and eyes, she knew what was happening in the basement. Deep red lips. Dark eyes, giving her something of a gothic appearance, but not quite. Eye lashes thick with mascara. And eyes enhanced with dark makeup. Pippa worked on herself slowly, carefully, expertly. But most of all she worked on herself with no hurry or no concern. She wasn't in a rush to get the worse done. She wasn't in any way phased by what she was doing or what she was going to do over the next few hours. The next few days. When she tried to choose a mode of dress for her work she came to a sticking point. She couldn't decide. Leather. Latex. Silk. Nylon. She had the choice of every conceivable fetish combination together with shoes and boots of all descriptions and all designs. She poured over the choices for what seemed an age. She wasn't bothered that she couldn't decide. She was having fun deciding. She was having fun doing what little girls did every day. Dressing up in mummy's clothes and high heels. Except Pippa never did that. She didn't get to do things that other little girls had done when they were growing up. She didn't get to do any of that shit. But now she could. It was like Pippa was transported back in time sometimes. Just for split seconds. Like she was remembering why she was here in this house with the two petrified people in the basement.

Pippa and Delores weren't exactly matched in size. But she could have mixed and matched and adapted. In the event she went with simple. Completely simple. Hold up stockings of the sheer and expensive variety for her extraordinary long legs. And the highest stiletto fuck-me-pumps that Delores possessed. In fairness to the older woman she had some stunning shoes and the size

9

was about right. Pippa had spent most time choosing the shoes. Once she had chosen the barely black sheer stockings she spent what she might have described as the time of her life choosing the shoes. It was like she was playing. Making up for lost time. Making up for that time she should have had when she was growing up but didn't. In the end she chose simple, black shiny patent court shoes. No ankle straps or anything to spoil the line of the legs. Or detract from the length of the legs. Pippa had stood in a full length mirror, naked except for the stockings and the heels. She had placed one hand on one hip and splayed her legs. She looked good. More than good and she knew it. She gripped her hair, pulled it back and banded it into a high, tight pony tail. That seemed to add to her height. Seemed to add to her effect. The effect of Pippa! Pippa the female sadist.

Pippa was hairless from the neck down – she had been for a long time. Ever since she could remember. It was the vulnerable in Pippa that saw her face change every so often. Like a shadow passing over her face. An expression change but just a slight one. Like as though she was remembering. Remembering things that she didn't particularly want to remember. But also a resignation in there as well. Like she was resigned to having these memories invade her head space from time to time. Like there was nothing she could do about it and she just had to accept it. But at the same time it didn't mean she had to like it. Just accept it. She always got a weird feeling when she was all but naked like this. And whenever she looked in a mirror like this, she always tried to focus on the spot between her legs. That spot. And what had been taken from her all that time ago. She always shuddered when she thought of that. But she had to go now. She had to go back down into the basement. She had things to do. People to see. People to 'see to'.

Pippa's generous breasts had swayed as she came back into the basement room. Both Max and Delores had held their breaths as they heard the key turn in the lock

at the top of the stairs. And then as those stilettos had descended the stairs they had looked at each other. Neither of them would be able to say that the feeling they got was a good one. Quite the opposite actually. And then they had just looked as the tall, pony tailed Pippa had come back into the room. They had looked at each other again. As though they couldn't quite work out what the fuck was going on. Like what did it even mean that this Pippa bitch was now naked except for stockings and heels? Did this mean that she was more vulnerable? Certainly she would be. Certainly Delores thought that way, being a woman and knowing how high heels fucked up a woman in more ways than one. But then the notion again being repelled by common sense. Pippa was the one in control. The situation didn't say anything other than this woman was in control, total control.

"Bet you'd like to fuck me now hey Max?"

Pippa had posed in front of the prose Max. She knew that penetrating her would be the last thing on his mind. She knew that the pain he was feeling from the ball kicking and kneeing would still be very much in his mind. Sexual desire would never have been as far away as it was at this point. But she had made her point.

"Delores, it's simple. I want you to stay on the chair, hold your hands behind your back, over the back of the chair. Interlace your fingers and keep them like that. Sit on the chair with your legs spread wide. As wide as they will go. And stay like that. Stay liked that until I tell you otherwise. Whatever I do to you, stay like that. If you move from that position, for any reason, I will remove one of Max's testicles, here in front of you. I'm not going to ask you if you understand because I know that you do. I know that fear and despair help to focus the mind on what is important and what is vital. So I know you understand."

Pippa spoke in her almost emotionless way as Delores adopted the position that she had been told to adopt on the chair. It was like as though she had been

trained without being trained. In Pippa's world there was no need for training. Obedience and submission came through from fear and shock. Pippa didn't do 'training'. What she did was simple destruction. What she did was destroy people. And she did that because of what she had been through in her early life. The full extent of what she had been through might never be known. But from how she lived and what she did to other woman, it could maybe be guessed at.

"If you're a good girl Delores this little bit of what I have planned for you will be over before you know it. On the other hand, if you're a bad girl, it will go on a bit. If you're a bad girl it will go on longer than it might have otherwise."

Pippa had crouched in front of the seated Delores and she had reached up and held the woman's lower jaw in her upturned hand. Cradled the lower jaw between her thumb and forefinger. Delores was visibly trembling. Her face, her whole face was visibly trembling and Pippa's hand was doing nothing to stop that trembling. It was as though Delores knew that she was about to enter the worse time of her life ever. And that she didn't know when, or if this time was going to end. Whatever she thought, it wasn't good. There was no good slant on her thoughts. There was nothing positive that she could take from the thoughts that were going through her mind. But Pippa knew that. She knew exactly what was going through this woman's head. She knew this woman was on the verge of being fucked psychologically. And she knew that she controlled this whole process. The whole shebang she knew was down to her.

"You've got a pretty face Delores. I'm sure you've been told that lots of times hey? So, what I am going to do is make it a little less pretty. I'm going to change it a little bit. Not that this is part of my bigger plan for you both. I will just work better if you are less – let me think, if you are less 'pretty' if you get my drift?"

Once again she was using words to inflict damage

inside Delores's mind. Like a precursor to the beating she was about to inflict on the older woman's face. Delores visibly sank on the chair more. She had seen what Pippa had done to Max. She had witnessed the sort of violence that she was capable of. And now the focus was on her. And there was a noise. It was a little time before she realised that the noise that she could hear was coming from her own mouth in the form of a whimpering, dreadful sobbing.

One might have expected a begging and a pleading for the beating not to ensue. But there was none of that. It seemed bizarre, almost unthinkable that this woman was not begging for some kind of mercy. Or that Max, who had watched and listened to the exchange between his own deep seated sobs, hadn't pleaded on Delores's behalf. He was her partner when all said and done. And he was the man. Man might have been stretching it a little. He said nothing. The focus wasn't on him. That was all he knew. This girl woman thing, this chameleon like ageless woman wouldn't be inflicting anything on him for the time being and inside he was grateful for that. It seemed inconceivable that this woman, this Pippa, in stockings and heels and nothing else could have inflicted this control and this fear and this dread in this couple. But she had. She absolutely was the one in control. She had the couple frightened for their lives. She had them pretty much frightened of their own shadows. She cradled the jaw of Delores and she turned the older woman's head one way, then the other. She did it slowly. Like she was looking at her from all angles. Almost like she was planning her angle of attack on that pretty, pretty face. And then it started.

CHAPTER TWO

REWIND 4 – the past

There was city noise but it was in the distance. A long way in the distance. Like a distant buzz. Or a hum. That was it. The hum of the city in the distance. Kind of weird really – that hum. It provided some kind of warm comfort. Telling this girl that there was some life somewhere. Other than this place she had been taken to. That there was some sort of life elsewhere. Maybe that life would come get her. Come save her or something. But then she had given up on being saved any time soon. She should have been able to rely on her mother. Her mother should have protected her but she didn't. Mother was too interested in getting her next fix. Her next high. It was her mother who was allowing these things to be done tom her by this man. Hell, it was her mother who had seen her little girl as a bargaining tool. And a bit of meat that she could trade with in return for her crack fix.

She tried to ignore the pain. But the fact that she was losing control of the contents of her bladder was a reminder of the pain. Her feet were off the floor. She was suspended and she was naked. She was always naked these days. Being naked helped get her mother the fix. But what this man was doing to her paid the most crack. She was suspended by her wrists. Her feet 'just' off the floor. And she was peeing. She was losing her bladder contents. The urine was gushing. But it was gushing to her thighs. There was a urine spray but that spray was saturating her upper thighs and the pee was running down the length of her bare legs. When it got to her feet, and to her toes it was dripping under her. Her legs were not secured together or anything so she was free to move her legs. Scissor them or whatever, but that was all she could do. Oh and she could curl her toes. She did a lot of that. She did that in response to the pain that was being inflicted on her. Every time a glowing cigarette end was

14

offered to her flesh she curled her toes.

The thing was that her toes were only just off the floor. The tips of her toes were only just clear of the floor. They were so close to the floor in fact that it was natural for her to try to reach the floor with them. Try to take some of the weight off her wrists. Her hands had gone numb. She was used to that feeling. Numb hands. It was a familiar feeling to her. This man liked her hands to bare the weight. She would never know why that was the case. He was a sick turd of shit, she knew that. One day she would get the opportunity to end it all and she would do that. She would end her life in this world. She actually thought that. That she would kill herself. That doing that had to be better than having to deal with this pain and torture and abuse for the rest of her life. That was the problem. She was thinking in terms of 'the rest of her life.' She couldn't see past this thing she was in. She kept having flash backs to those men in the car. And in that underground place. She had come out of that on top. But she couldn't kill everyone that abused her. Could she? She couldn't demise everyone who had designs on her young body. It had to be her fault. It had to be her fault that men wanted to do these things with her and to her. Why else would they do it? Why else would her mother let this man do this to her? She could kill him, in some way. But then what would she do with her mother? Her mother was the reason behind this latest shit. Her habit. Or the maintaining of her habit. Would she kill her as well? She couldn't do that. She already had flashbacks to what she had done to those men one at a time. What she had done had sickened her and yet at the same time she had got something from it. Hearing that ring leader begging for his life after he had seen when she did to his accomplices had fed her with some kind of buzz that she would never be able to explain or describe.

It was all her own fault. There was something in her, something in her makeup in her DNA that made others want to do these things to her. It had to be her

own fault. If she was 'normal' then people wouldn't do these things to her. But that was it – she wasn't normal. She had never been normal. Not for as long as she could remember at least. There had been that 'uncle' when she was really young. He had given her the creeps. But even he must have known that there was something about her that made people want to hurt her. He had never touched her. Not like that. Or hurt her. But it was like he knew. He used to look at her in that way. A way that told her that he knew she was a bad one and that bad things had to and would happen to her. It was like he looked at her the way he did knowing what the future held in store for her. Like he was no different to the people who hurt her the way they did. He was weird. Weird to her in a lot of ways. But then he was there one day and gone the next. He had vanished off the scene and she never saw him again. Her mum never talked about him. Never even mentioned him. Which was a surprise given that she had seen her mother slip her mouth over his cock more than once. Just through a crack in the door. Like the door to the bedroom had been left open like that deliberately so that she could see. Like this man, or her mother, or both of them were subjecting her to some kind of 'primal scene'. Something that would stay with her for a long time. Something that would stay with her for life in fact. It was because of what she had seen those time, her mother sucking cock, that she knew what to do when the time came. In a way she had learned to suck cock off her mother. Her mother had in a way, passed down her skill set to her little girl. It was just a fucked up thing. Completely fucked up.

She had often thought about asking her mother what had happened to her 'uncle'. She knew he wasn't her fucking uncle. Just some pervert that her mother had picked up and had been on the scene for a while. Then gone.

"That hurts please don't do that."

Her mother had taken a drag on her cigarette and

across. It burnt because the girl flinched. She flinched and she whimpered. One might have thought that she would kick her legs with that burning sensation. But she didn't and in a way that was the sad thing. It was like she was accepting the torture. Like she accepted that it was what happened to her and she couldn't do anything about it. At least she couldn't do anything about it for the time being. At some point she would. Like she had dealt with those men. It had all come on top of her then. The pain. And the feeling of exclusiveness in that place underground. She would never be able to describe what had come over her. It was like a red mist that had come down over her eyes. And it had been like she was having an out of body experience as she despatched the men one at a time. It had been so quick that they hadn't be able to do anything about it. It had been like lightning quick and yet at the same time, through her own eyes it had been like something happening in super slow motion.

It was sad the way she just hung her legs, held still whilst her mother burned her with that cigarette and then the next one. That acceptance – the resignation. No one who saw that would be able to get the sight out of their heads. This poor girl. And the black man – he was getting ready for something else. He was getting ready to do something else to her. She knew that. He had watched the mother with a big white toothed smile and then he had begun to undress himself. Slowly revealing the hugeness of that cock again.

Somewhere near there were dogs barking. Big dogs. Every time they barked, the girl's eyes would shoot over into that direction. The direction where the barking was coming from. And there was this fear in her eyes. A terrible fear. She didn't want this man to bring the dogs in. Not again. Something had happened before for her to look like this when those darks barked. Something unmentionable had happened and it had to do with those dogs. It would take the darkest of minds to go there. To go to a place where what could have happened with this

18

girl and with the dogs, could come to the fore. For it even to be imagined what could have happened. Sometimes it was better not to go there. Not even in the mind. And yet from the look of utter fear on the girl's face when those dogs barked, she couldn't help but go there and remember what had happened. Then the man was there, right next to her hanging, limp self. And he was whispering to her.

"They can smell you, you know, bitch. They can smell a bitch in heat. They want you again. That's what they want. They want to bitch you, again. You'd like that wouldn't you, hmmmm?"

And he was licking her face. She hated having her face licked. She hated it since those other men had done it. The ones she had killed. And what he was saying. She hated that even more. She could feel this man's breath washing over her face and she could feel his words eating into her psyche. She whimpered. At first it was like a noise she didn't understand or know. That noise of her own whimpering. Then she got it. Then she knew it was hers. And that whimpering was like a sobbing from someone beyond the pit of her tummy. From beyond her soul even. She let another gush of urine loose as those thoughts of the dogs, big Ridgeback dogs having their way with her again. She had to think of something else. She had to try to think of something else at least. Something that would take her mind off those dogs. Trouble was that by this time the dogs, three of them were howling. She wondered if they could really smell her. And if they could smell that she was a bitch in heat. She hated that thought. Being bitched by those dogs, again. No she couldn't think of that she had to think of something else. She had to get those thoughts and those memories out of her mind.

The big black man could help her with that though. He was ready now. He was going to fuck her. He was going to fuck her as she hung by her wrists like that. She was at the right height for fucking. He could jack her up

onto his hips and he could fuck her pussy and he could fuck her ass. Yes he had decided this time, that it was the right time for her ass to be fucked for the first time. And he had decided that he was the one who would do it. A nice tight ass wrapped around his thick vein ridden cock. He might even get mum to suck him clean after her had fucked her daughter's ass. Now there was a thought that made him smile wide. She would do anything, literally for her next fix. And all to the soundtrack of those barking dogs. Except the barking had morphed into a whining and a scraping. Those dogs trying to get out of wherever they were. Trying to get to where the girl was suspended. Oh god she didn't want that. No she didn't want that. Not at all. She willingly lifted her long tapered legs and hitched them around this man's hips. Just so that if the dogs came they wouldn't be able to sniff her legs. They had done they before. Before they had mounted her. Hey had sniffed her legs and she had had to deal with that sensation. The cold snouts against her flesh. All of that before they, well you know before they did her.

The girl made some kind of noise. It wasn't so much a cry as a scream. The man slipping his cock into her tight cunt. It hurt. It hurt a huge amount and the more she tried to ease her own suffering the more it seemed to hurt her. If she squeezed on that cock, if she squeezed herself onto it then it hurt her more. That pain, deep indescribable pain because there was something so big in her, so unnaturally big in her that it was telling her central nervous system that it shouldn't be there. And that was right. It wasn't right that this big black man be fucking this young girl like this. Especially not like this. Mum was on the floor, under the lifted, jacked up legs of her offspring and she was still smoking. Still smoking and still blowing on that cigarette end before reaching up and dragging that red hot ember across the underside of her daughter's thighs. That was making the girl twitch. Making her twitch further onto the cock that she was impaled on. And that was the thing. She was impaled on

that huge cock. Her mother would have been able to see her little girl's most private and sensitive flesh wrapped around that cock. To her it would have looked like the flesh was about to rip. That cock, the hugeness of it would have stretched her lips to the maximum and it would have just looked that at any time, the flesh would rip and she would bleed.

"Keep burning her bitch. I want this little bitch to twitch on my cock. Keep burning her."

The man was hissing in some kind of deranged lust with no thought of this girl or what he was telling her mother to do. He didn't care. It was just all about his own pleasure. The pleasuring of his own giant cock. If that meant that this woman had to burn her little girl to make her twitch, to make that sensation through his cock better for him then so be it. And she did. Mum did it because she knew at the end of this session she would be given a bag of crack that would last her for forty eight hours or so. And at this time that was all that mattered to her. The bag of crack. She was in withdrawal now already. But at least she was earning her next fix. That was all that mattered to her was her next fix. It didn't matter to her that her one and only girl would be the one to really suffer so that she could get that fix. And because of her state of mind she was thinking how she could better please this man.

If she burned the area around her ass – inside the cheeks, between the cheeks then it would hurt the girl more. The constant pressure and friction there. The constant pressure and friction making those cigarette burns raw. They would hurt. Maybe later as a little extra she would put some salt on them. Rub a bit of salt into the burns. Yes that was a good idea. That way this big black man would be even more pleased with how the girl was suffering. Maybe he would give her a little extra for showing some imagination. Maybe she would getting some extra crack for showing a little initiative. She liked that thought. She dragged her glowing cigarette and

down the valley between her daughter's cheeks as the man was pistoning his cock in and out of her. Ironically the mother was disgusted at how wet and dripping the girl was. How could she be aroused? There was no thought that it was just the girl's body reacting to what was happening to it. There was no thought either for the fact that at any time now the man would remove his cock from her cunt and offer it up to her even tighter ass. That was to come.

CHAPTER THREE

Now

They were just light slaps at first. Slaps like Pippa was testing the water. Like she was getting her distances right. Just light slaps to Delores's face. With the palm side of her hand, and then with the back of her hand. Just back and fore. Pippa stayed down, crouched down on her heels. There was something wrong about it. Something sexual about this woman in her stockings and heels. Just lightly slapping Delores. It had sexual overtones that were not good. The whole thing was sexual. But there felt to be something wrong about that. Like it shouldn't have felt like that. There shouldn't have been this sexual element to it but there was. It just seemed wrong that this sexual woman has this hold over this couple. Max by this time had stopped sobbing. His balls hadn't stopped aching though. And there was a deeper hurt inside him. He was all but silent except for a heavy breathing as he was forced really to stand, prose like he was and look over the ensuing scene. In actual fact he wasn't forced to do that at all. But he couldn't take his watery eyes off Pippa in the early stages of beating his partner up.

Max would never be able to say what it felt like to watch that. To have to watch that. There were things that he didn't understand. Like why or how Delores just sat and took it. How she didn't defend herself. Oh, he had heard the instructions and the warning of what would happen if she moved or changed position, but as those slaps got harder and harder, and as Delores's head was rocked from side to side, it seemed beyond belief that Delores didn't try to move, or alter her position even if only to lessen the effect of the slaps that were steadily increasing in intensity.

There was something sickening about the sound of those slaps as well. In that low ceilinged basement, the sound of hands and fingers on facial flesh was almost

sickening. Pippa stayed almost squatted on her own heels until she was in a steady rhythm. But then she got up. It was like she couldn't get enough leverage when she was down low like that. It was like she couldn't get enough energy behind the slap. Being down there had been alright to start with. That meant she good get her distance. She could get the measure. But by the time Delores was sobbing with each slap, Pippa needed to stand up. And in standing the beating paused just a little. Just enough for the older woman to catch her breath. Pippa cradled the older woman's jaw again and tilted her head up. Like she was inspecting her work up to this point. There was no serious damage. Not yet. Just little red marks around the cheeks. Around the eyes. Those eyes appearing puffed up a little but that as much to do with Delores's crying than the slaps.

Pippa's first slap after she stood up marked an upward trend in intensity. It was a back handed one that rocked Delores so much that she almost fell off the chair. If she had have been knocked off the chair then that wouldn't have been held against her. The momentum of that slap would have been the cause, not the woman herself trying to protect herself. It seemed inconceivable that this woman was not 'allowed' to protect herself. That if she did it would result in something worse happening. It was an almost 'sad' sight. This girl beating this woman who was not even making the attempt to protect herself. The severity of the beating to her face moving her on the chair. Moving and rocking her head. The sound of those slaps sickening. Like a flat hand hitting wet flesh. Every so often Pippa would stop and cradle that jaw. Almost like she was studying her work of art in process.

"Not nice is it Delores, being on the receiving end?"

Pippa's voice almost smoky, husky, provocative as she spoke down to Delores. And then beating her again. Holding Delores's jaw at arm's length. Turning it a little and SLAP. Holding it there, letting the woman sob then turning it the other way and SLAP. Holding it again.

Then three or four slaps in quick succession. SLAP SLAP SLAP. The backhanders targeting the areas under Delores's wide eyes. Those eyes had been gorgeous eyes. Big, like pools. But now they were marked. And they were closing. Pippa targeted those eyes intently for some time. She knew what she was doing. And Delores just sat, let her head and her face be guided and posed in readiness for the beating it was getting. Everything about the scene just seemed sad and melancholy for some reason. This woman being beaten like this. It wasn't right. Nothing about it was, or seemed right. Every so often Pippa would stop and she would step back and take in a deep breath. Something seemed to alter about her. The chameleon at work again. Her stature seemed to increase. And there was almost an arrogance about her stance in those stockings and heels. Like she was now in her natural habitat or something. Like she was at last in a place in her mind she could call hers. But it all seemed so wrong though. Like nothing seemed to be right about this scene. This scene couldn't be right not from any angle it was looked at.

Delores, as much as she could was just watching, just looking at Pippa as she beat down on her. She stayed on that chair, her hands and fingers clasped behind her back. God that was awful, seeing that. But more awful, the expertly applied beating that her face was getting from the woman in stockings and heels. The sexualised beating of a woman by another woman. There was something so wrong about that. And yet it continued. It continued until the slaps became more than 'slaps'. Those slaps slowly turning into closed fist, wide swinging punches. It didn't get any more wrong as the beating progressed. Both eyes of Delores almost closed. It was like Pippa had stopped short, only just short of those eyes closing altogether. They were swollen and they were 'almost' closed. But not quite. It was like Pippa didn't want to blind Delores with her own swellings. At least not just yet.

Pippa cradled the sobbing woman's jaw in her hand again and tilted her up so she could see.

"Not quite so pretty now Delores. I'm beginning to like you more now. Now that you're not so pretty."

The next closed fist punch was to the nose of Delores. There was an almost sickening crunch and then a spray of blood. That blood, prayed out over Pippa's legs, soaking into her stockings and spattering her thighs above the stocking tops. Another blow to the nose underlined the damage that had been done there. Max had dared to utter,

"Oh for gods sakes."

Even as the words were coming out of her blabbering mouth he knew he was doing the wrong thing. He hadn't even meant to say it loud. He was just thinking aloud. If he had known what was going to happen next he would have made a concerted effort to keep those words to himself. Delores delivered another blow to the cute upturned nose of Delores and then she moved round to Max. The stiletto'd kick that she delivered to the already fucked balls of this man was accompanied by a similar crunch that Delores's nose gave out. It was a sickening crunch that would leave anyone who heard it puzzled as to where exactly the 'crunch' had come from. That kick had been so lethally accurate and hard that the damage could down there, to Max could only have been furthered. The air and the wind gushed from him and was accompanied by a scream of pain that was so terrible that anyone would cringe. Even Delores cringed and she was suffering enough herself. Pippa didn't cringe she just moved in close to Max and she licked the side of his face before whispering,

"If I want your input I'll get you to give it. Until that time, shut the fuck up."

One could never be sure if it was the kick to his balls that made Max piss himself. It had to be something to do with it. That kick. That crunch and then the gush of

a piss showing that he had lost control of his bladder. Then Pippa returned her attentions to Delores.

The woman was seated still. Her eyes were swollen, almost closed. Her nose was bleeding. And there was nothing confident about her body language. She had been denied any dignity. Or more to the point she had had her dignity taken off her by this girl woman. The body language added to the sadness of that scene. Somehow, even knowing what this woman and her partner had done to this girl who was now controlling the scene, one felt sorry for her. There was a sorrow for her because there was no sign of an end to the ordeal for her. It was clear that this was not a simple case of someone gaining revenge in a schoolgirl way for something bad that had been done to her or said to her. It was clear that Pippa was on a different path of revenge, like a furthered and more advanced revenge than the simple playground stuff.

By the time Pippa's fist crash into Delores's jaw, she was having to hold the woman up. She wouldn't have blamed her for slipping off that stool with the force of the blows. The thing was that she didn't want her to fall off the stool yet. In Pippa's mind, this woman sliding off the stool to the cold stone floor would mark the end of the beating and she didn't want to do that. She wasn't done yet. And she really wasn't done yet. There was a noise that was coming from Delores but nothing decipherable. It wasn't clear if her jaw was broken, or dislocated. Or both. But it was fucked. Split lips, bleeding. And one final hard, super hard punch to that jaw to try to even up the distortion. And that was the one then sent her skidding off the chair to the floor.

"Get your ass back on the stool Delores. Now!"

Delores looked stunned but she reacted to the voice of Pippa and she dragged herself onto the chair. It was natural for her to adopt the position again and she went to slide her hands around the sides of her hips to the small of her back and Pippa watched. She was silently

27

impressed. She could have some real fun with this woman. The problem with Pippa, when she was in this place, when she was in this sub space of hers was that she was seeing her mother. She was seeing her mother in Delores's place. That face she had beaten was her mother's face. Everything she did was kind of like she was doing it to her mother.

"That's right slut. Fingers interlaced."

Delores could only assume that she was going to be beaten more. Except she was wrong about that. Pippa circled the chair. She liked the 'slump' that she had forced on Delores. That suited her more. It suited Pippa more that this woman who had been the driving force behind the hurt applied to her, was less filled with dignity and more filled with fear, and indignity.

"It's ok sweetheart. I'm not going to beat your face any more. For now. You've had enough of that, I can tell. I don't want you to think being with me, like this, is all about pain and beatings. It's not all about that at all."

It was like another person was talking and not the Pippa who had designed and executed that severe and merciless beating to Delores's face. Not to mention the kicks and the knees to Max's balls. Her voice, her tone was different. It was like it had changed in an instant. Like someone else inside her had come to the fore and was being very nice now. Very kind. But that caused all sorts of shit to kick off in Delores's head. It played with her senses. It fucked with her mind. The good cop bad cop thing. And yet that kindness didn't stop this woman from cowering on the chair she was perched on the edge of. Her face was trembling and then she was crying. Not just crying but sobbing bitterly. No grown woman should have been sobbing like that. No grown woman should have a reason to sob like that, except maybe for grieving purposes. But this wasn't that.

Even Pippa's body language had changed. Even that had become softer. Like she all of a sudden had a softer edge to her. Like a soft focus filter had been fitted to the

lens. But what kind of ruined that filter was that this woman girl, chameleon thing was splattered with Delores's blood. And despite that soft edge, there was still something brutal about this thing that was going on. Something achingly brutal about this whole scene. This woman, this Pippa had caused carnage in that basement in that suburban house. The weekend was barely half over and she hadn't finished yet. Nothing about what was happening in the here and now said that this girl was finished with the couple just yet.

"It's ok Delores. Its ok. I know you're hurting. But you deserve to be hurting after what you both did to me. But it's not all about pain. It's not all about you hurting."

Pippa was down again, sitting on her own heels, and she was reaching up with both of her hands. And with her thumbs and forefingers she was lightly gripping Delores's nipples. Very lightly. Just tugging on them, not to hurt them but to encourage them to fill and bloat. Encourage them to erect. Just squeezing her fingers gently and then releasing. Squeezing then releasing. Pippa got in closer so that she was pressed against the trembling legs of Delores. Using her as support she could use her hands and her fingers more effectively. She could spread her fingers and take in more of the woman's breast flesh. Not in a nasty way but in a kind way. Delores didn't get it. The expressions of puzzlement across her face told that she didn't get it. Or more to the point that she was confused. That this girl was confusing her. This was a girl that could inflict pain in the blink of an eye and with intensity that was paralysing. And yet now, there was this utter sensualness coming from her. Like a kindness that she was grateful for. There was no reason for her to be grateful to this mad bitch who had beaten her senseless. And yet that was what she felt as Pippa stroked and caressed her breasts. Both breasts. It was like she was grateful for the sensual side of this girl. Grateful that this girl was not hurting her some more. There was even the slither of the feeling, of the thought

that she could kick herself for feeling grateful like this. But she was. That feeling, the one that she should kick herself melted away with those strokes and with the caresses of her breasts.

"I know. I know what you're feeling Delores. Just relax. Go with the flow. Let it all go."

If she was meaning to fuck with Delores's mind, then Pippa was succeeding. Delores tried to lick her lips. But they were cracked and bleeding and swollen so she couldn't feel her own tongue slipping over them. But there was something else. Something that was just too wrong for her to believe. This woman was sexually arousing her. She had beaten her senseless and now she was sexually arousing her. Those feelings, those sensation starting at the very tips of her nipples and then spreading down through the core of the nipples and to the inside of her breasts. Those sexual feelings stronger than she had ever felt before. Delores would have been one of those people who thought that she had experienced most things sexual. And yet with what she had been through, and now this, would be blowing her mind. Had blown her mind. She was hearing Pippa's words and those words were sinking into her psyche and tumbling round there. She couldn't believe that it was the same woman talking to her like this. Giving her pleasure like this. But yet at the same time she knew it was. She knew, in an instant that this woman could cause intense pain and intense pleasure within the same second if she so chose.

"I'm going to make you come Delores. I'm going to make you come just by focussing on your nipples. And you are going to experience an orgasm like you have never experienced before. Just by touching and stroking and caressing your nipples. And then, once you have come, I am going to hurt you some more."

Surely it would have been better for Pippa not to tell Delores what she was going to do? Surely she should just get on with it for best effect? But no. That was the

point. Letting the older woman know, telling her what she was going to do. Introducing the light and shade, black and white at the same time. Causing this woman's mind to melt a little bit more. Letting her know that it was alright for her to revel and wallow in the pleasure for now, but that very soon she would be plunged back into pain so terrible that she would rather block it out. Or rather, try to block it out. It was the whole point of what Pippa did. She was playing with this woman. Good cop bad cop. Pleasure pain. And taking parts of her mind and twisting them. Twisting and squeezing and distorting them. It was what she did. Delores would have considered herself an accomplished sadist. But now she would know that she was just a learner. And not a very good one. She would be learning what being a sadist was really all about. Or rather she was learning what it was to be on the receiving end of what a true, and truly accomplished sadist could do. This was mind fuck, this was body fuck and this was twisting another person at the higher end of the scale. At the higher end of the pay grade.

By the time Delores was sitting on that chair orgasming, she was unable to think anywhere near straight. Actually she was unable to think at all. All she could do was absorb that pleasure, that intense and absolute pleasure that Pippa was letting her have. It was part of the kindness of Pippa. At least that was about the only thing that Delores could think. That this girl was being kind, intensely kind just before she had to get sadistic again. But it would be some time before Delores would get it. Get it that the fact was that Pippa's kindness and her sadism were one and the same. She flooded that chair. Flooded it with her own juices. Part of her learning process. Part of THE learning process.

CHAPTER FOUR

Now

There was a mixture of noises coming from Delores. Grunting and heaving for breath. She had just been made to come on an intense scale. One couldn't say that she had been permitted an orgasm. Or that she had been given pleasure. Those descriptions just seemed to contradict what orgasm was all about. If anything, Delores was 'inflicted' with that orgasm. A juddering tsunami of pure and undiluted pleasure that was bordering on pain. It was a whole bunch of sensations that Delores's central nervous system wouldn't have been able to decipher. Not properly anyway. She had held her hands behind her back, gripping her own fingers tightly as Pippa had worked her nipples. That was all she worked was her nipples. Just rubbed them carefully all round the aureole. At first she didn't make contact with the nipples at all. Just teased them. Teased them by circling them. Just running her finger tip over the speckled raised aureole. Very lightly. Almost hovering her fingertips there. Just very lightly around and around. Those fingertips barely sliding over the surface of those speckles. And all the time, Delores catching her own breath. Catching then holding. Catching then holding. Her cracked, bleeding lips trembling. Trembling a lot because she was trying to make sense of what was happening to her - that pain and then this. This pleasure or this kindness. She wasn't sure what it was. Whether or not it was either. She didn't know and her way of dealing with that was to tremble. Tremble and whimper. Yes that was what she was doing, whimpering. She couldn't stop that wet whimpering sound from coming out of her mouth. It was like something that was always there. It was just there pouring out of her damaged, cracked and bleeding mouth.

Maybe there were words formulating in her mind. It

was doubtful though. And even if there were then they didn't make it out of her mouth. It was like she had been struck dumb whereas she wanted and needed to ask questions. She needed to know what was happening to her. She needed to know why this woman had hurt her so much and now was giving her this pleasure. Her feeling grateful for that pleasure seemed to be a given. She didn't know that she didn't have to feel grateful for anything. That if anything all she needed to do was feel hate for this girl. Whoever she was whatever she was. But it didn't work like that. What Pippa did to her victims. It didn't work like that. She was playing with Delores's mind as much as she was playing with her sexuality. She was playing and she was twisting. And then she was playing some more. She brought each of those nipples to a painful erection. A painful erection that wasn't painful at all. The throbs from the base of the nipples working their way through, all the way through to her clitoris. But there was no contact with the clitoris. None at all. Just those invisible strings tugging and pulling at the hidden ends of the clitoris. The nerve endings inside the flesh. Where the clitoris nerves erupted from the flesh. Those nerve endings that couldn't be reached. Couldn't be scratched. Just all of her sexuality being reached and being manipulated from the nipples. How could this girl do this? How was she doing this to her? After she had given her so much pain, how was she doing this to her? How was she doing it?

Delores slid around the seat because she had wet the seat. With that manipulation of her nipples had come the wetness. Like a dripping, slow leaking wetness that didn't stop. Like a tap that had been turned on but couldn't be turned off again. And she was sliding round in her own wetness. She was still clinging to her own fingers behind her but Pippa didn't stop her from sliding round in her own produce. In her own mess. Pippa would have known about those intense feelings and sensations. She would have known all about that slow

build up to orgasm. And she would have known that it would have been melting Delores's mind. Melting it and pouring it over what was left of her psyche. She didn't hold that against this woman. She wasn't doing what she was doing by accident. It was a skill that Pippa had. An unnatural skill but a skill none the less.

And then, there it was. Just a unified swipe with both thumbs across respective nipples. Just again, the lightest of touches and Delores was coming. The orgasm had built up behind both nipples, right under the surface – the unscratchable orgasm. And then on the point of release that built up pressure was transferred to the clitoris. And the moment that happened, the absolute split second that that happened, there was what can only be called an explosion between Delores's legs. An explosion of pure pleasure come pain. If she had been asked to describe it, or explain it, all that would have come from her cracked bleeding lips would have been indecipherable nonsense. It would have been unlikely that any words would have formed in her mind as it melted. There was just this 'thing' that took her over. That took all of her over. This thing that was like an orgasm she had had in the past. But was countless times more powerful that one of those could ever be. And the noises that she made at the height of that orgasm were almost not human. She slid down the chair and was almost lying on it as that super orgasm rocked through her. And as she orgasmed, so Pippa rubbed those nipples very lightly. Ever so lightly. At the height of the orgasm those fingertips were barely touching the nipples but then Pippa leaned forward and she blew over the nipples. Just little blowing breaths right across the tip of each nipples. Delores screamed then. At the very pinnacle of that orgasm she screamed. And then... and then nothing.

The orgasm vanished as soon as it appeared. Or as soon as it had manifested itself.

"You enjoyed that. Didn't you, slut?"

The edge had come back to Pippa's voice. As if in a

flash that kindness and that sensuality had gone again and the other one was there. That other nasty Pippa.

"You owe me now. You owe me for that pleasure I just gave you. Do you understand, slut? You owe me!"

There was more of that edge. More of it that worked its way into Delores's mind. She nodded. Yes she understood.

"I can't hear you slut. You owe me don't you?"

This time Pippa reminded Delores about the slaps to her face. She back handed the woman. Not hard. Just enough to make her flinch. Just enough to petrify her all over again.

"Y-yes. Yes I owe you."

Delores would have wished she didn't have to get those words out but she did. They were demanded of her.

"In fact. I want to be repaid now. This very instance. Now!"

Pippa's words had got harsher and harsher. The tone had got harsher and harsher and by the time that she was bending each of the nipples at the base she was almost spitting between gritted teeth. It was another level. Pippa had unleashed sadistic horror in an effortless way. She had barely broken sweat and certainly hadn't even breathed hard. But now she was seething it seemed. Or was this another of her acts. Another of the things she was using to twist this poor woman's mind just a little bit more. It was an act. Delores had become, to a point, desensitised to the sadism so she needed it to be upped a little more for it to have the same or worse effect. She whimpered as her nipples were banded with strong tight elastic rubber bands. They had already bloated when she had orgasmed. That had receded from that but now they were back up again. Pippa had twirled the bands around her fingers and then applied them to each nipple. Feeding them down the stems. All the way down the stems until they gripped the base. That constriction then feeding the nipples with more blood. Feeding them and making them hard again. Hard, swollen, erect and

elongated. And then Pippa produced one of Delores's own canes. A steel cored, tightly braided leather cane in the fashion of a dressage whip. She slashed it through the air and it made one of those noises that put anyone on edge. A mix between a whistle and a slash. Not one or the other, but both.

Pippa didn't begin the caning of the nipples straight away. She didn't want to. She didn't need to. In the first instance she needed those bands to do their work fully. She needed the nipples full, engorged and bloated. They would be bigger then. They would be a bigger target for the whip cane thing. Not that Pippa needed anything to help her accuracy. But she wanted them full and heavy so that the effect of each stroke would be fully and totally felt. That would take a few minutes. And for those few minutes she would let Delores sweat on it. It was all good though. She was letting it all weight heavy on Delores's mind. The pleasure. That mind numbing pleasure and now the pay back. This was all good for Pippa. This was what she did the best, play the mind game. Not that there was anything wrong with her practical sadism. She was an accomplished sadist. She should not have been but she was. She seemed too young to be that good, or that bad at what she did. But what it seemed didn't matter. She was accomplished in all manner of ways.

And then she started. She didn't warn the woman she was going to start. She just casually adopted a position and did mental calculations. Then there was that slash and whistle as the end of the whip cane thing sped through the air. The very end, the very thin and of that cane coming into mortifying contact with the nipple. About halfway up its stem. First just that whistle and slash and then the CRACK as contact was made. And what a contact! There was a split second where there was no noise. The whistle and slash, and then the crack and then the 'nothing'. A split second in time when everything seemed either to stand still or proceed in

super slow motion. Delores's face seemed to be in that super-hyper-slow-motion. It must have been the time it took for the message to get to the brain. There might have been a delay because Delores was already in meltdown. So a delay of another few hundred thousandths of a second and then there was the wall of noise. That wall of noise coming from Delores. Her beaten, bruised, bleeding, swollen face screwed up and this pure noise coming from her as the full effect of than cane and its message to the brain hit home. And before she had stopped the scream from that the cane was whistling and swishing and slashing again and there was that CRACK again. This time the whip end, the cane end, making contact with the other nipple. Like the first, right across the top of it. Halfway down the stem. That crack of the contact almost a sickening thing. And then the strangest thing of all. As if this poor woman was letting out two lots of noises with the same voice box. That seemed an impossible thing, but it was true. That first scream not having faded and died and there was the other one at full volume and at full tilt. This time her face screwed up more as the double pain but home. Both sets of pain doing their best to break this woman once and for all.

Delores had been through enough. She was on the edge of something. That nipple caning kept her teetering there. Pippa inflicted another thirty or so strokes of that cane to Delores's nipples. All the time warning her,

"Keep your hands behind your back bitch. Move them and you'll be sorry."

As though the woman wasn't or couldn't be sorry enough as it was. Thirty or so strokes then she simply stopped. Stopped slashing that leather braided cane through the air. The noises coming from Delores had changed. There had been those soul searching screams. But as the nipple whipping had proceeded, as the nipple caning had progressed the screams had altered and changed and morphed into other wet noises of despair.

By the time the last stroke had been applied there was this almost 'grunt' from Delores. It wouldn't have been a grunt that Max would have recognised from his partner. She had been the ultimate feminine in his eyes. The ultimate woman. Sex on legs for sure. She had done things for him sexually that other women wouldn't have been able to get close to. And yet in that basement she had been reduced. Reduced was a good word for her in this place. Reduced. Beaten, bleeding and swollen. But then once that nipple whipping was complete, once it had been done and dusted all there was from her was silence. There was the steady breathing. Like she was absorbing, or trying to absorb the pain that she had been inflicted with. But otherwise there was nothing. She simply sat on that chair. She didn't move. She didn't raise her head to look at the room – to look at Max. Or to look at Pippa. It was like she was afraid to do that. Afraid of the eye contact just in case it spurred on more of the same. Or some of the worse yet to be inflicted on her. It was like she was in some kind of silent survival mode. It was what her body, what her mind was telling her to do. In the absence of any other solution, there was nothing else that she could do.

And then there was Max. He had surely been subjected to the worse pain a man could be subjected to. Repeated kicks and knees to the balls. Not just random ball busting. But premeditated and vicious kicks and knees that would surely have rendered this man incapable of reproducing. Indeed as he stood there, legs splayed, hands hoisted above him he had silently, painfully reflected how much less of a man he 'felt' since this girl had done what she had done. There was just 'something' in his psyche that told him he was less of a man now. There was something 'broken' down there and he knew it. It was something beyond the pain that he felt. The pain that was there all the time. Just something that told him – that let him know he wasn't a man any more.

"I can be nice to you as well you know Max. I can

38

be real nice to a guy like you. I was taught to be you know. To be nice to guys like you. Oh I had good, good training in being nice."

The sultry Pippa was back. All legs, stockings, heels and that smoky voice and red lipstick. That was the cause for alarm bells in Max's head. He had just seen through the haze of his own tears, the results of Pippa's being nice. And then the payback. But then he was supposed to see all of that. He was supposed to see and hear it all. It was supposed to have that effect on him. It was supposed to frighten him half to death if he hadn't been frightened half to death as it was. There was always method in Pippa's madness. And him seeing his partner suffering the way she had, and now being under 'threat' of this girl's niceness was not a good thing. It wasn't a good thing at all. He tried to talk. Tried to decline Pippa's 'kind' offer. But nothing sensible would come out. It was like his ability to speak normally was playing tricks on him. All that came out was rubbish in no decipherable words.

"No no you ssshhh now. Let me be extra nice to you. I can be you know. Extra nice. All for you."

It was like Pippa could and had read this man. She was moving into him and she was being gentle with his cock. He thought he would get away with her niceness because he was convinced that he would not, or could not work down there. But he was wrong. She had damaged him just enough to ensure his reproductive system would not work anymore. His balls were all but fucked. But there was something about the brain that didn't let go of the desire. And it was the desire that Pippa was using as she took his cock gentle and lifted it, then rubbed. He flinched a little as she lifted it. Like he was expecting it to hurt. He had been convinced that if he lived, he would never touch himself down there again ever because it would surely hurt a lot. More than a lot. But then he felt his cock coming to life. And that was the thing. It was coming to life. And the desire in him was

alive, for a short, a very short time there was desire and his cock was hard. Rigid. His balls still ached. They still more than ached, like there was a deep hurt in there somewhere. A deep hurt right inside his manhood. But his cock was hard. Maybe he should just live for the moment and let this woman have her way. What did he have to lose? Nothing.

"That's a good little bitch. Good little bitch."

Pippa repeated herself as though emphasising what she was saying. And she spoke as she gripped that cock and rubbed it to its fullest most obscene erection. That was the same cock that had been inside her. That was the cock belonging to the man that had raped her repeatedly. And now she was rubbing that cock and she was bringing it up again. She was pleasuring him. He wished in a way that she wasn't doing what she was doing. Anyone would bet that was what he was wishing. But he didn't have a say. All he could do was go with the flow. That was what Delores had done – she had gone with the flow. And now she was sitting on that chair in an amount of pain that can only be thought of in terms of nightmares. And she was like a mute. Like a frightened mute. Would he end up the same as her? Would he be petrified out of his wits and afraid even to look up from the floor? But then the thought that surely she had done the worse that she could possibly do to him and that there was nothing else she could do to surpass that. Maybe she did just want to pleasure him. Be nice to him. Maybe she thought that he had suffered enough and there was nothing else to do to him. That it was time that he had some pleasure. Maybe she was just being kind to him. Not!

CHAPTER FIVE

REWIND 5 – the past

By the time that cock was offered to her ass the burns were letting their full effect be known. It might have been that the sting of those cigarette burns would take the focus off what was going to be out and out pain throughout her rear entrance. But that wasn't the case at all. Not at all. Mum had stabbed and dragged cigarette after cigarette around the girl's buttocks and her upper, outer thighs. By the time this monster of a black man was lining himself up to slip his cock into her tight, tiny ass he had dug his fingers, and his finger nails into those burns. Not in a deliberate action – rather just to get a good purchase. A good grip on this girl so that he could fuck her deeper and harder. There would come a point when one would feel sorry for this girl. But it wasn't when she was being fucked hard and deep. It would be before that. At the point when that massive, smooth, red bell end was offered to her ass hole. Mum would have been helpful as ever. She would have changed her pack of cigarettes for a bottle of baby oil. She would have been making sure that the entry was smooth and unhindered. It wouldn't have entered her mind, at any point, what she was doing. How she was helping, assisting to abuse her only daughter like this. That she was helping the process of this awful black man be inside her only daughter. By using that oil on her. Oiling the cheeks, the inner cheeks and her crack. At one point pouring the oil down that crack so that it ran over and into her ass. That oil making sure there was no resistance. The only resistance was the pure size of the cock head and the smallness of the girl's ass hole. The actual physical smallness of that hole.

This man could rub his cock head all over that area before he entered her and he did. Using the oil to lubricate himself as well as keep her lubricated. Just

wedging it between those tight little ass cheeks. Except it was wedging it in there it was sliding it in there. Slipping it between the cheeks and then over the hole. Not into the hole straight away but over it. Slipping it and sliding it. The way he could do. He wouldn't put it into her until he was ready. Until he got bored with slipping his glans over that delicate soft, well-oiled flesh. His oily finger running over her oily flesh and then his fingertips seeming to seek out and dig into the cigarette burns. If anything that baby oil irritating those little burns and cigarette trails.

"Daddy's gonna fuck your ass now girl. Because you've been a bad bad girl."

Mother hissing her words. But not just hissing them – almost reciting them in a sing-song nursery rhyme kind of way. It made the words and what they meant sicker and more grotesque. This man wasn't the girl's dad. So why would this woman, the mother of this girl say those words? It was part of her knowing what this man wanted and needed. It was part of what she knew about his perversions. She knew what turned him on and she was pandering to those whims. Pandering to the whims of this out and out sadistic pervert. Even when her next bag of crack was assured, she was still thinking ahead. It was like she was several steps ahead of herself already. Her knowing what turned him on. What words and deeds turned him on? Now that the crack was assured she might have been feeling that pang of guilt for what she was doing. What she was providing this man with. But there was none of that. None of it at all. Rather she was spurred on by events. Spurred on by the event itself. And it was an event. The noise alone made it an event. Maybe an event from a nightmare – like a noise from a waking nightmare. That noise didn't belong in the normal, serene world. It belonged in a nightmare. It belonged in that other place.

He hadn't announced that it was time for his cock to be slipped into the girl. He had rubbed that giant of a bell

42

end over her time after time and for a long time. Just teasing that tight little rosebud of an anus by slipping the oily bell end over it. As he had done that he had fingered her burns making her twitch. Then he had dug those fingers in to the burns twisting them. Making her twitch more and harder. That was what he did when he entered her. He had found a relatively bad burn and he had dug his finger nail in and twisted. She had whimpered out and she had twitched. He liked that. He liked the way she twitched against his cock. Liked the way her flesh felt against his cock head as she twitched with the pain from that burn. And he had used that twitch and had altered his angle just slightly. Very slightly altered his angle. And then when she was in mid, multi layered twitch he shoved himself forward. Her legs were around his hips and she was still suspended by her wrists. She would have had no chance during which to protect herself or avoid that pain. She was completely at this man's mercy. And at the mercy of his surreal cock.

The noise when it came was like a wall of noise. At first it seemed detached from the girl. There might have been a split second when one would think there was no way that a girl, let alone this girl could make a noise like that. But as quickly as it was detached, it was re-attached again. And there was this wall of noise coming from the girl's twisted mouth. Her facial distortion told only one thing, that she was in an agony that she didn't understand. The black man had been deliberately slow in the way he had entered her ass. There would have been a way that he could have done it quicker. The pain would have been sharper more intense but for a shorter time. He chose the long hard way. Just teasing his cock to the tight raised rose bud asshole of this young girl and then pushing. But not pushing right in. just pushing slightly – getting the stretch underway. Just putting it in a little bit. Making the girl spasm against his cock. Making her ass spasm around his massive bell end. As she spasmed she tightened more. That made the pain more. Then he

moved out again, more or less taking his cock out of her but not quite. Just letting her relax a little bit. Ease that pain before he shoved in again. This time slipping more into her. Him repeating that action time after time.

All the time though he was just teasing her. Teasing that oiled ass. When it came time for him to put the fullness of his bell end into her altogether was when the wall of noise was at its height. When it was at its most intense. At the point where that cock clicked past her sphincter the pain was so bad that this poor girl visibly tightened. Every muscle in her young body seemed to tighten and spasm. And one might have thought this man, as evil as he was would have showed some compassion at that point. He had what he wanted. His cock was inside this girl's back passage. Surely he could show her some mercy. But no. No, that wasn't the case at all. He took the time, seconds, maybe a minute to feel her tight round him after he had put his enormous bell end into her. But then once that moment had passed. Once he had got over that as a thrill he pushed on deeper into her. He gripped her hips and he pushed on more inside her. And as he did that she screamed out more. And louder. That pain when he had clicked past her sphincter renewed and intensified even more as the thickness of his shaft stretched her anal tunnel. All the way inside her until he was nudging the bend in her colon. Then he was fucking her. He was fucking the core of her femininity. And then he was flooding that core of her. Flooding her with his hot fresh semen. It wasn't like she wouldn't have been able to feel that flooding of her back passage, it would have been like she was being given a thick creamy enema. It would have added to the pressure up inside her. Big gobs and globules of semen coming out with his out stroke. That semen dripping to the floor underneath her.

There had been a point – just a split second. When the noise coming from this girl was at its height, when the mother looked up at her. The mother tilting her head

slightly as she watched her girl in the most pain she would ever have experienced. Just at that precise moment there might have been some remorse there. That mother love finally coming through, at last. But it was short lived. There one second then gone.

She was still dripping as mother and nameless black man talked about the next stage of this girl's demise. Not demise in the truest sense of the word. Although one might think that she would want to be dead. And not until he had fucked her cunt either. He had to do that – to feel the tightest, warmest wettest flesh around his cock. She would wish that she was dead. Or would be killed. She was as numb to her mother as she was to this man. It was like she wasn't her mother at all. It was like her mother was this other woman. Just an accomplice of this man. Which of course she was. There was this disconnect with her mother. And there was this acceptance, this resignation again. It made the scene sadder. It made it stark and raw and cruel. The man threw mum a bag of crack. She had been paid in full for what she had done, and what she had provided so far.

"I want her clit hood taken off. And I want the tip of her clit taken off. Do you understand, bitch? There's more where that came from if you can do this for me. It's important that YOU do it. That I see YOU do it."

Mum was nodding agreeing even as she was prepping the crack for a hit. Heating it up in a stainless steel spoon with her lighter. Getting over that, breathing it in. That would do for now. That would do until she got time on her own later. When she got time on her own she would heat more of the rocks. Melt them down and then inject the liquefied crack direct into her veins. That would be the big hit. That would be the one that would send her into the stratosphere. And that would be her out of it for days on end. It might be a week or more until she came down from that one. If she came down at all that is. For now she had to remain at least a little compos mentis. There was a promise of more crack even before

45

she used up this latest batch. She had to stay on top of things until she got the extra. Then this black pervert could go fuck himself. It would be ok with her girl. She would make it up with her and it would be ok. She would understand. She would understand that mum had been in a dark place. And that she just needed that one final extra special hit. That beautiful hit and fix.

It showed what a crack head this woman had become. Wrapped up in her own fucked up world and not even knowing what she was doing to her own daughter.

"Yes, yes I can do it. I can take that clit hood off. And the clit tip. Trust me. You give me more of this stuff and I can do this and more."

Mum getting further and further into it. Committing herself further and further. And promising to damage her daughter more in the name of the drug that she needed so badly. This man so perverted and so sexually deranged that probably he was beyond any form of help. A man who was so fucked up that one might wonder at his own history and his own life. What could have happened to this man in his life for him to end up this way. It's true some people are just evil. Born evil. But usually there was some kind of explanation. Some kind of happening in the life of someone evil. Such a mystery would never really be solved. It would never be solved in the case of this man anyway. Events would take a turn eventually and this man would be no more. Events would take a turn and this girl's mother would be no more either. But not yet. Not just yet.

Seeing her hanging there, offering no fight, no resistance to what was being done to her was a sad sight. It should have been a sick sight. But it was just sad. A girl so resigned to what was being done to her that she just hung limp. Suspended by her wrists, knowing that she couldn't do anything. And knowing that no matter what words she chose to plead with, they would fall on deaf ears. Or not so much deaf ears, but ears not

listening. Those ears attached to people, her mother and this man who were on their own agenda. The mother needed that final crack hit –that would see her through until she got clean and made it up with her daughter. Not! And this man, after the next big hit of sexual euphoria. In a way he was worse than a crack addict. This was a man plumbing the depths of human sexuality for his kicks. Even plumbing beyond the depths.

It was never going to be a pretty or a neat clitoral circumcision. The mother had stabbed her own hand with the scalpel the black man provided even before she got near to that sacred place between her daughter's legs. She had sniffed that crack and was in the process of dealing with the fallout from that. She had pinched the clit of her girl. Got it swollen, got it erect. She did that on the man's say so.

"Get it nice and hard, it's easier to do the hood then."

Like he had done this sort of thing before. Alarmingly like he had done it before in fact. But he was right. The tips of those eight thousand nerve endings poking out, beyond the hood. Providing a focal point and a guide around which to use the scalpel. And immediately before she did it, mum was focused. And steady. As steady as a non-medical professional and a crack head could be. And then she used that scalpel. There was no cry or no scream. Strangely, almost bizarrely, there was nothing. No sound that came from the girl at all. Nothing. There had been a little squirt of blood as mum inserted the tip of the blade at the base of the hood. Where the rolled hood flesh folded into the clitoris itself. There hadn't been even any tensioning by the girl. It was like the message hadn't got straight to her brain. Or maybe like the message that her most intimate sensitive flesh was in the process of being butchered had gone on some kind of detour or something. Her legs just hung limp. She was simply accepting. Complying. And mum, strangely focused. As focused as she had been for

47

a long time despite her addiction. Twisting her hand slowly as she followed the base of the bundle of nerves that made up the clitoris. Slicing through and peeling away that flesh. Peeling it away from itself. Mum working slowly, almost methodically. It was as though the inner surgeon in her had come out and taken over. This was something that she had to get right if she was going to get that final supply of crack that would give her such an immense hit that she would be able to come off it with no problem at all.

That's how deluded and fucked up this woman was. Fucked up and deluded to think that she could 'just' come off crack as soon as she had had that final hit. She even handed the circumcised clitoral hood to the man. Placing it in the palm of his wide open upturned hand. Him smiling. A wide almost beaming smile as he looked at that flesh. In a few hours that clitoris hood would be in a small phial that he would wear on a leather lace. That little bit of flesh submerged in some kind of solution that would assure its longevity. Like a trophy around his neck. And it didn't matter what the fuck this girl went through due to her loss.

"Use this. Do her clit tip."

He had handed her like a shaver. Like a medical shaver. It should have been easy to use. But there had been something about the noises that the girl was making by this time that sort of disturbed the mother's work flow. And her focus. It was like finally the massage of that scalpel slicing through her most tender flesh had got through. It was like finally it had got where it was supposed to go. And yet now here was mum, pinching the clitoris itself between the thumb and forefinger of one had – getting it back to its fullest erection before with one swipe of the medical razor thing, she took off the tips off that bundle of nerves. First the hood, gone. Had this girl just had the hood removed, she would have been consigned to a lifetime of enforced sensitivity down there. Almost like a fate worse than death. But

48

then the tips, the very tips of those nerve endings. The business ends as it were, gone! Her sexuality taken away from her. Taken away from her by this woman who was supposed to be her mother. And by this man who had to be everyone's worst nightmare, except his own. By the time the message had been redelivered to her brain the noises that were coming from her were different noises altogether. Like a low guttural moaning. A moaning that was wet and dripping from her mouth. Looking down the length of her, her legs kept bending at the knees. Lifting her ankle back under her thighs. As though she was trying to relieve herself of the throbs of pain from the scalpel and razor cuts that had been applied. And that was it, they were 'throbs' of pain that would stay there. That wouldn't go away. Mummy was planning for her future. It was going to be happy ever after. She just needed that final hit of super crack and then she would be fine. She would stop taking the drug – she would get back on track with her one and only offspring and it would be all ok. The man was planning his next step as well. His ultimate sex trip. His ultimate buzz. It involved extreme sadism and it involved murder.

The thing was that the girl, hanging, her sexuality mutilated, was planning as well. The thing was that her thoughts, her plans were more lucid and clearer than those of the people that had been torturing her. Her plans simply contained murder. The murder of two people. Just like those men that had done those things to her. These two people, including her mother, had to be dead.

CHAPTER SIX

Now

The kicking, and the kneeing to his testicles had done damage. That much wouldn't take a medical professional to point out. There was that deep seated pain that wouldn't go away. Right inside, not in the testicles themselves but beyond them. Deeper. And there was that ache that wouldn't go away either. It just wouldn't go away. More than the usual ache associated with a knock to the balls. It had been like that at the start, but then then ache had seemed to recede deeper and hide somewhere else. Somewhere deeper. And when there it hadn't gone away. It hadn't faded or died. It was like it had gone somewhere deeper to live. Like it had gone somewhere deeper to make his life from this point much worse.

"Mmmm this isn't right either is it, hmmm?"

Pippa was using her husky smoky voice. She had got Max's cock hard but she was holding it. Like she was holding a 'thing' between two fingers. The thick cock was hard. It was hard, she had given him an erection. He should have been pleased about that. But there was something deep inside that told him not to be. He didn't need to be told if the truth was known. He didn't have a good feeling about this. He was still looking through tears. The same tears that Pippa had brought to his eyes when she had tortured his balls. Delores was on the chair, still. She had the blank look on her face. And that body language that spoke of her fear of moving even a muscle unless Pippa said that it was ok. But that was the thing, Pippa didn't say anything. She didn't give permission for anything and so Delores was left in some kind of weird petrification on that chair. Except for the trembling of course. She could tremble without permission. She could tremble because it was a sign of how the sadist had affected her. And that was ok. It was

50

ok for the sadist to see signs of what she had done on others.

But that didn't help Max. Pippa's attentions were now on him and he was wishing that his cock would have stayed soft and useless. He had this deeper feeling that with his cock hard, this woman was going to do all sorts of nasty things to him. He couldn't help but look on the bleak side. Maybe there was good reason for that. He looked down. He was right. It wasn't right. There was an erection, of sorts. But it was like a broken erection. Somewhere along the line in that kicking and kneeing that Pippa had given in with no mercy, she had broken his cock. For some odd reason Max, instead of wondering about his life, and the immediate future, was trying to work out how it had happened. He should have been whimpering for some kind of mercy. He should have been trying to work out a way out of this thing. But he wasn't. He was looking down at his own cock held between this woman's thumb and forefinger, and he was trying to work out how it had got broken. Or when exactly that had happened. It was broken. His thing was broken!

"It's broken isn't it hmmm? It's all bent up and broken. We can't have that now can we, hmm?"

Pippa was using that word that Max had been thinking. Broken. She was right it was broken. But for some reason he didn't want to talk about that with her. He had this feeling that if they talked about his broken cock, that there would be more pain involved. Not just a little bit of pain, but lots of it.

"We need to straighten it out, don't we hmm? Get it nice and straight, nice and hard. The way it should be don't you think?"

The fact was that no he didn't think that. He didn't think that they should straighten it out and make it hard again. He had more than the feeling that that would involve more awful pain. One might guess that it was as well he couldn't imagine the actual pain that would be

involved. He nodded his head, found himself agreeing with Pippa simply because he was afraid of her. There was no other way that it could be described other than he was afraid of her. He felt less of a man because of the fact he felt afraid of her. That was something else she had taken away from him. She had taken his machoism away. He had revelled in the way he could petrify and fuck their victims in the past. Him and Delores had made the perfect couple. The perfect partners in crime in what they did. Charm younger girls and women in bars and then take them back and do things to them. Do things to them to the extent that these women and girls would never tell. They would never talk about what had happened to them. That was the effect that Max and Delores had on others. And on the victims that crossed their paths. How things change. How things can change so quickly!

But this was a different thing. This was a different kettle of fish altogether. Pippa let the cock dangle as she went to look for what she needed next. It was as though she knew what she needed was here, she just needed to find it. That was the thing about Max and Delores, they were wealthy and they had hobbies. Those hobbies in sadism. They had become fully equipped even though their experience didn't stretch to using most of the stuff they had equipped that basement with. When it came down to it this was a couple who dressed basic abuse and rape up in a fetish and BDSM cover. They had been just perverts using fetish as a cover for what they did to their victims. But now they had become victims themselves. Now the tables had been turned. They had fucked around with the wrong girl at that club that night. There was no way they could have known how the night, or how the weekend would end. There was no way that they could know how this whole 'thing' was going to end. Now they just had to go along for the ride. It might have been a ride they didn't want to take. If there had been any other option then one had the feeling that they would take the

other option to that ride any day of the week. But there was no option. Pippa was controlling it now. Not them. They were now the victims in their own sick game.

"You don't want me to straighten your cock, do you?"

Pippa put on some kind of spoilt brat voice and then pouted as though she was being denied her own way by a parent. Max wanted to shake his head and say, fuck no, I do not want you, you fucking mad bitch anywhere near my cock. In fact I don't want you anywhere near me, period. And further to that, let us the fuck go.   But whatever he was thinking, it didn't come out like that. In fact it came out nothing like that at all. And the words than just about came from his mouth he could barely believe.

"Of course, of course I want you to fix my cock. Please, please do straighten it. Please."

It was the effect that this woman girl had on her victims. There would have been victims. Max and Delores wouldn't have been the only ones. Or the first ones. This was a girl who could create a carnage not of this world. And she must have got that skill somewhere and somehow. It was the sort of experience and skill that one only got 'on the job' as it were. The words that came from Max's mouth were like not his words. And yet at the same time they were his words. Like deep down inside he didn't want to disappoint this woman by saying the wrong words. The classic saying what she wanted to hear. Or rather saying what he thought she wanted to hear. Basically deep down he was afraid of this woman. Afraid for his own life. And he would say anything to get him through.

"Yes good boy. Good boy. I knew you wanted that same as I want. I just knew it,"

It was as though Pippa was gloating. As though she had gained some kind of victory in hearing those words coming stuttering from Max's mouth. What Pippa was carrying didn't look to be good news for Max. it would

take him a look or two through tears, and through the maze of fucked up thoughts that was his mind, to realise what she was carrying, and what it meant for him. It was easy to see that exact point when realisation dawned on him though. There was like a catastrophic change in expression on his face. Any colour that might have been there was drained like on an immediate basis. And then there was the haunted look. The look of horror that was overlaid by this haunted look. It wasn't a good thing. He had agreed that his cock needed to be fixed. Needed to be straightened. Other than the bad, bad feeling, there had been no thought about how that fix would be achieved. Other than the feeling that it would involve another ordeal, or involve an extension to the ordeal he was already going through, there had been no thoughts at all as to how the fix would happen.

But now, the stockinged and heeled Pippa had found what she needed to make it happen. What made this worse was the fact that this ultra-attractive feminine creature was splattered and streaked with blood already. It made her look brutal. She was beautiful yes, but there was this sense of 'violence' about her. An underlying fear that this woman was capable of more, much more than even she had carried out so far. And what she was carrying back to Max let on even more about her. That she was capable of inflicting pain on a micro level. On a medically accurate level.

Supplied by a company that specialised in medical equipment. Medical equipment that was modified from the ground up for BDSM and fetish purposes. A 'sound' that would be fed into the cock head of Max and pushed down, all the way down his urethra tube. A normal medical sound was not a pleasant thing to have to experience for medical purposes of which there were many. There were many applications, mostly exploratory, in medical circles. And yet this sound, the one that Pippa was carrying was a 'version'. That it was only a version was where the similarity ended. Stainless

steel shell and sleeving gave this instrument its medical credentials. But the core of it, the actual sound, bore no resemblance to the real thing. It worked, or was operated more like a corkscrew. Like a corkscrew used to pop the cork from a bottle of wine. The sound was intricately shaped like a cork screw. One look at this thing and one didn't need to be told how it work, or what was required to work it. One didn't need a drawing to be made in order to explain how it worked. It was one of those things, given the conversation that had happened between the two, one just knew what was going to come. There didn't need to be a warning that it was not going to be pretty. There did not need to be a warning that it was going to be nasty. It was just something one knew as soon as one saw that 'thing'.

"I know, I know it's going to hurt. But you know Max, people like you need pain in their lives. People like you, and the slut over there need pain in your lives. And you need to feel grateful that I am helping you straighten this 'mess' out. You need to be real real grateful."

There was no doubt that Pippa sounded like a maniac. She even looked like one. A maniac in stockings, heels and lipstick, streaked and splattered with blood of her victims. Max had to remain bondaged for what was to happen to him next. The pain and the psychological damage that was involved was surely too much and on a different level to make him stay still, and do as he was told like Delores, and not protect himself. The bondage had to stay. Yes he would strain and he would scream. But that was ok. This couple had way too much money. They had never needed complete and utter sound proofing in that basement. But they had got it installed anyway. Because they could. And now it was their own sounds that they were containing and not the sounds of distress and despair of their victims. It was like that karma. What goes around comes around.

Pippa took Max's cock like it was that bottle of fine wine. Ok it was like a bottle that had seen better days.

With the knowledge, or with the fear, the erection, as bent as it was, had dwindled a little bit and so Pippa used her hand and her fingers to coax it back up. Max for the second time, wished it didn't work. But one had the feeling that this woman could make it work by whatever means. If it didn't work though, maybe she would have abandoned her plans to 'fix' it. It was all hopes beyond hope really. The mind playing tricks. The mind contributing to its own decline. Pippa took the cock, rubbed it to its fullest erection again, and then she paid special attention to the cock head. The huge mushroom that she had felt batter into her cervix and her colon time and time again. She squeezed it a little bit. Not to hurt it but just to open the pee hole and then she fed the little corkscrew shape sound end into it. A hollow tube fashioned and shaped into that corkscrew. Tiny and micro machined. It looked like it belonged in a horror film. Or some sick snuff movie. It looked like it belonged in this scene. It looked like that because it was meant to.

When Max screamed he didn't sound like a human being. Rather it sounded as though some poor animal had been trapped and was being tortured. It was a time when dignity was no more. If truth be known, Max had lost his dignity when his balls were being beaten, kicked and kneed. This was way beyond the final straw for him. Pippa didn't work quickly. It was as though she were stretching it out for as long as she could. As though she were stretching out her own pleasure for as long as she could. Screwing that sound down into Max's cock head. She would pause between each twist of the sound's handle. And she would look at Max − like she was studying this man at his most basic. At his most base. His screams, if they could be called screams, were timed to coincide with Pippa's 'twists' of the little handle. Pippa gripped the bent cock shaft with her free hand − like she would a bottle of wine. And she fed the sound down slowly, twist by twist. And as she did that, she was

straightening the bend that she had inflicted in it. At one point, and during one 'twist' of that handle, there had been a spurt of blood. That blood had poured over her hand but she had acted like it hadn't happened. Max's scream had been more intense then. The same sound, trapped animal scream, but more so. Delores watched. She watched her man suffer but her face was expressionless. It was as though her having no expression was akin to her not moving a muscle in case Pippa was angered in some way. That didn't make sense either. Pippa hadn't shown any anger at all, in any way. That was the worrying part. There was no seething anger. There had been no point at which she was acting in any form of anger. And that she inflicted the pain and the torture that she did without that anger or madness, was very worrying indeed.

As Pippa was straightening that cock out in her own imitable way. A long way from that house, in a city apartment there was a party happening. A party for beautiful people. City people. Champagne bottles, empty ones, turned upside down in ice buckets were all over the place. As were the bodies. Some collapsed in unconsciousness. Some in a semi-conscious state. Some people were still drinking despite the sun rising outside from the east. On a deep, plush sofa there were three people. Two women and a man. Even they looked worse for wear but they were talking.

"It's weird. I usually hear from Delores at the weekend. Even if it's just a text message to say hi. But I haven't heard a thing. Her phone is dead. She hasn't been on social media at all. Even Max is quiet. It could be nothing but I've got a bad feeling about this. I don't know why I've got a bad feeling. I just do. I'm gonna leave it a few more hours and then go out to the house. See what's going on. It could be that they've flown to Monaco or something. They do that sometimes. But they usually tell someone. Or let one of us know what they're up to. And

they can never resist one of those selfies from the window seat of a plane with the Monaco in the background as they come in to land. But nothing. I don't understand it. And I don't like it. It's just not like them."

The woman, Grace, had spoken. She had said her piece and then sat back recrossing her legs. Long legs that the silky dress she wore floated over and away to reveal yet more leg. She would have been a woman that Pippa would have been interested in. Snobby, educated and with that dismissive attitude that Pippa detested in other women. And yet there were the signs of caring in there. The signs of emotions that Pippa just loved play with. It was the kind of emotions that she had had once. And the kind of emotions that she had had played with, and destroyed once. Yes she would 'get on well' with Grace. In more ways than one.

"Maybe they're just coked out of their heads or something. It wouldn't be the first time they've done that. Locked themselves away after a long hard week, called their dealer and coked themselves up to the max until Monday morning. I'm sure it's ok. Grace you know how they like to do things off the cuff and unexpected."

The man's voice trailed off. That had been Bret – another city wanker who didn't really give a flying fuck about anyone except himself. Like he said the right things but didn't really care. He would have been the sort of guy who would have learned that Delores and Max had been murdered in their own beds and wouldn't have flinched. Life goes on and all that. He swigged from a flute of half empty champagne and sat back. His eyes trailed up the length of Grace's crossed over leg. His mind was on one track. Later, maybe after lunch he would fuck Grace. She had been asking for it for some time. Flirting and dropping little innuendos. She wanted it and so would get it. She would get it with interest. The three sat and didn't say anything else. Grace was deep in thought. Something was troubling her. Call it feminine intuition.

CHAPTER SEVEN

Now

That cork screw sound was twisted slowly down and down. Pippa had pulled that stool up – the one that Delores had been forced to stand on for her beating. And she sat on it. She wanted to savour this torture of this man. She wanted to be comfortable whilst she was screwing that sound down inside the middle of his cock. To do that she had to be in close and she had to be steady. It wouldn't be an understatement to say that every single 'twist' of that sound caused the kind of pain that this man hadn't had to deal with before. It was the type of pain that didn't have a type attached to it. It was the type of pain that was in a type and class all of its own. One look at Max's face would tell anyone that the pain was constant and it was intense. And it was the type of pain that didn't get easier to bare the further down that sound was screwed. It was a pain that started bad, like the kind of pain that the victim would think couldn't get any worse. But it did get worse. With every twist or half twist of that sound there was a barrage of sound that came from him. And that barrage of gut wrenching sound became the soundtrack to what was happening in that basement of that suburban house.

Pippa had been deliberate in getting the most out of the torture of Max. There had been no hurry to do that. No hurry at all. She knew what would hurt. And she knew the kind of utter pain that would make the man who had raped her, wish he was dead. And that was the thing. Max wished that this lunatic of a woman would finish him off every time she twisted that sound deeper into his manhood. He wished she would just finish him off. And eerily, it was as though Pippa was reading his mind.

"I know what you're thinking Max. I know what you're wishing. You're were dead right now hey? Just so

59

you didn't have to put up with this pain any more. Just so that you don't have to feel this."

She punctuated her words with another twist. And for that underlining twist she put just that little bit more effort into it so that it hurt just that little bit more. What that corkscrew sound was doing to the tube and inside of this man's cock can only be imagined. Or perhaps not. The strangest thing – the weirdest thing though – Pippa had got that cock hard again. Bent but hard. And despite the pain that erection stayed intact. Despite that intense, indescribably pain, that erection stayed intact. An erection under such terrible duress and intense pain. Inside the cock, the tube was being opened up against itself. That tube being expanded and widened. The widening of that tube being the source of the pain. With every screw the sound moved down further. Not a lot. Just a little bit. It was why the pain, the torture could be held out for so long. It was why it could be extended and drawn out. It was why Pippa could make this torture last as long as she did. She could make it last as long as she wanted. It was the type of torture that she didn't need to constantly work to keep up the pain levels. She didn't need to do that because the pain was instant and it was constant. That pain didn't reach a crest and then die off with each twist of the wrist. It crested and stayed there until the next twist was carried out by this female sadist.

And that was the thing, this woman twisted with a relish. There was something in her eyes that would tell anyone that she was enjoying what she was doing. But that wasn't solely it. She was enjoying, she was reaping the rewards, some kind of perverted twisted rewards out of the absolute pain she was causing this man, but she was doing it in a controlled way. Doing it in such a way that she got the absolute most out of it. Like she knew how to get the most out of it. And that was the chilling thing. That she knew how to hurt this man in such a complete way and that she could enjoy it at the same time. A lot of sadists would feel the need to record and

playback their worst atrocities in order to get the most out of them at a later date. Later time. When the worst was done and dusted and the cleaning up had been done. Then they would play back in high definition video what that had done. Then they would get the buzz. Then they would get the most from it.

But this isn't what Pippa did. She didn't record and hold the evidence for posterity. She didn't need to do that, she had become so accomplished that she wrung the most out of it without the need to set up cameras and then the added hassle of recording it all. She was a sadist who lived for the moment. A sadist who got the most – got the total buzz from what she was doing at the very time that she did it. Maybe it was why she got away without being caught for so long. This was a woman who acted with impunity and who could cause the most absolute carnage and then simply walk away after it. She could do that because there was no evidence left. There was nothing that could be traced to her. Nothing that could be held against her at a later date. She did what she did and then she walked away. She simply walked away leaving that carnage behind her.

She twisted that sound down into Max's cock, and into his masculinity with a relish that defied any kind of belief. She wasn't jumping for joy or anything like that as blood simply squirted. Her relish came through in her eyes. From her eyes. The way she got close to the cock. The way she wanted to be in close proximity, as close as possible to the flesh that she was torturing as she could. It was like she wanted to be in that 'space'. She needed to be in that exact space. And as she twisted that cock further and further down so it became straighter. So that bend, or that 'break' that she had created became straight again. She had broken it during the ball kicking and during the ball busting kneeing that she had subjected this man to and now she was repairing the damage, kind of. It was ironic what she was doing. She screwed that sound down and down. Let the corkscrew shape find its

own way down that tube with her helping hand twists. Pippa paused every so often just so that she could listen to the noise that Max was making. Like she was bathing in that noise. She guessed, no she knew that the sound was corkscrewing its way into his bladder. A few more twists and she could change the end of that instrument for electrical wires and battery connections. Then she would make this man make another set of noises. She would play him like a musical instrument. She would get noises out of him that no other sadist could get. She would get noises that would make Max sound less than human. And that was the point of what she did.

The level of violence that this girl could execute was unbelievable. The level of sexual violence that she could inflict without so much as batting an eyelid, or breaking sweat was just, not right. There must have been a point when this couple, this poor couple, whatever they had done, must have thought that this woman had been wired up all wrong or something. There must have been a point at which they thought they were being controlled and tortured by little more than a stunningly attractive monster. Because that was what Pippa was. She couldn't be anything else whilst doing what she did.

Delores hadn't been able to look up. She had been afraid to look up. Afraid that if her eyes made contact with those of this woman, then the attention would be turned to her again. She didn't want that. She wouldn't be able to cope with that. So she looked at the floor. Kept her eyes to a fixed point. But she could only do that for so long. Those noises that Max were making weren't his noises. Those were noises coming from deep inside. Deep inside him. Guttural noises that were wet and slippery and that slipped out of his mouth because they wanted to escape. Escaping noises is what they were. Every time his screams reached a peak, Delores shuddered. But she kept her focus on that spot on the floor. It was only when a droplet of blood hit that spit – hit that exact spot that she had her focus changed. She

wished she hadn't seen that blood spatter. But she did and as she did she brought her eyes up. And then what she was seeing was making sense. She knew then why Max was making those terrible noises. She knew why he was making the kind of noises that she had never heard him make before. To Delores they were not masculine, man like noises. It sounded like his masculinity, his manhood had been taken off him. Ripped away from him. It sounded that with every twist of that 'thing' a little more of his manhood was taken away. It sounded like this woman was bitching Max without him being impaled on any kind of cock. It felt to Delores that this woman was carrying out her own imitable brand of 'bitching'. She was a woman and Pippa was a woman. Therefore they had something in common. Delores thought like a woman and she could think like a sadist bitch. There was an understanding there. A pure understanding of what Pippa was doing here. One couldn't be sure if understanding this woman was a help or not. It might have been better not to understand. Might have been better if she was blind in some way. But she wasn't. She knew and she understood this Pippa woman. And because she knew and understood she was embroiled in a different kind of torture.

"You like it don't you slut? You like what I'm doing to him. To 'it'?"

It had been what Delores had been dreading the most. The eye contact with the female sadist. That eye contact coming like a shock from within. And then the realisation that this woman's attention was now on her again. She didn't want to suffer any more. She couldn't suffer any more. If she agreed with Pippa maybe she would spare her. But that was something that she didn't know. She knew and understood this woman to a degree, but she didn't know or understand how much more she would want her to suffer. Pippa had been as competent in torturing her as she had Max, so she was not a man hating lesbian who targeted or tortured only men for fun.

This was a complex mother fucker of a sadist who maybe could never be worked out even by so called experts.

"Y-yes. Yes I like it."

Delores's voice was tiny, small. There was fear and anxiety and despair dripping from her mouth with those words. It wasn't difficult for her to be convincing though because those nipples of hers, despite the caning, despite the torture, had retained an erection that was as abnormal as Max's erection under such duress. Delores's voice a quiet, mouse like squeak whereas before it would have been loud, confident, arrogant. Pippa would have been making mental notes. She would have been marking down in her mind how this woman had been broken. Making comparisons with how she had been when overseeing her rape. And how she was now. How she had been through the breaking process. Pippa smiled. She was a mess but she was a sexy mess. Nothing on except those stockings and heels that had belonged to Delores. They still belonged to Delores and yet at the same time they didn't. Somehow this woman Pippa had taken everything from Delores. Her dignity. Her pride. Her material possessions.

It was something that felt wrong and yet at the same time something that felt right at the same time. Those stockings, those heels, her flesh spotted and splattered with blood. A mixture of Max's blood and Delores's blood. She looked like a refugee from some kind of horror film. But at the same time she looked sexy. Oh so sexy. How sexy Pippa looked was the one and only thought that was in Delores's mind and she could have ended her own life because of that one thought, she shouldn't have been thinking like that, but she was. She was thinking this Pippa was so, so sexy. In a way she wished she was her. Or wished she could be like her. Maybe it was the inner survival instinct in her. Join forces with that woman and she would be saved from death. Or maybe saved from a fate worse than death. If

she became as one with her, they may become lovers, or something. Delores was thinking with her mind racing. All the time thinking that it was too late for Max – somehow she knew that his days were numbered. Even his minutes were numbered. She couldn't save him so she had to think about herself. Getting herself out of this utter shit that she was in.

Delores heard herself whimper from between her lips as Pippa stopped screwing that sound into Max's cock and came closer to her. And when this younger woman kissed her on the lips there was another groaning whimper, this time into Pippa's mouth. Pippa sealed her lips to Delores's and she pressed in. It was like she was feeding off that groaning whimper. It was like she was tasting it. Tasting the despair there. And then she was reaching between the open legs of the woman and she was stroking the slit. Delores's sex slit was wet and it was slippery. She could feel her own wetness as Pippa stroked and as she kissed her. She wished that she wasn't wet but she was. She didn't know what was going on inside her head. This woman had done terrible, terrible things to her and yet here she was wet. Sexually wet and slippery. Pippa ploughed her fingers through the folds of her sex lips and inserted them a little bit. Not all the way in, just a little bit. And Delores sighed into the mouth of the sadist again. And again Pippa tasted her. She tasted this woman and then she broke the kiss. She broke the kiss to whisper,

"I know you want to be my lover Delores. I can feel it. I know it."

Pippa's voice was smoky, sexy. Delores must have felt that she was making progress. That she was going to come out of this alright after all. Ok, she was hurt, and she would never be the same again but she was coming out of it. There was light at the end of the tunnel. She must have felt like it was going to be ok after all. That she would lose Max in some hideous way or other, but that she could blag it. That she could play this sadistic

65

fucked up bitch at her own game until she was in a position to get help. Until she was in a position to either destroy Pippa herself, or until she could alert the authorities in some way.

"Mmmmm yes. Yes please. Yes to be your lover mmmmmmmm."

Delores offered her mouth for Pippa to kiss again and the female sadist did that. She kissed her deeply. Very deeply. Pippa's tongue slipping in, all the way into her mouth and Delores suckling on that tongue. Suckling on it in that submissive way. A way that would tell the sadist that she owned her. That she owned this older would be sadist. And Pippa kissed like she got that. She kissed this woman like she meant it. Like she was along for the ride. Like she was along for Delores's ride. That kiss seemed to go on for an age. It seemed to linger and for some reason it seemed to be a tender moment. A more than tender moment between the two. And then she moved away.

When the closed fist blow came to the side of Delores's head and face, the older woman was immediately stunned. She immediately didn't know what the fuck was going on. She was almost knocked off that chair. She had been barely able to save herself from the undignified fall to the floor. And in that split second, for some reason she knew that she had been rumbled. She knew that Pippa hadn't fallen for it at all. That caused a shock to take over her entire body, and mind. And that shock was a deep seated one. All of her worst fears coming true at the very same time. She had really believed that she could see a way out. That all she had to do was play this sadist's game. Pretend to be her lover. Get herself into a better position to get away. She was convinced that it was all falling into place. And now this.

"You Delores are a cunt if you think I'd fall for your shit. I know about survival instinct and all that you see. I know what a person will do to survive. I've been there. I've done it. I've got the T shirt you cunt. And if you

think you are going to get out of this, alive or otherwise, you've got another think coming. I haven't even started with you yet. I'm dealing with Max because I want you to feel what he goes through before I come back to you."

There was that snarl in the voice of Pippa again. Not a snarl that manifested itself in any way across her face. Just one that came out in her rasping, almost hissing voice. She had been playing games with the woman. Lulling her into a false sense of security. Making Delores 'think' that she might get out of this thing. And then revelling in letting her know that that was not going to be the case at all. Delores just looked up at Pippa. She couldn't avoid that eye contact now. And Pippa's face was close to her own. The side of her face throbbed from the blow and she could feel the live swelling even as she looked up at Pippa. Their eyes were meeting and there was understanding there. Understanding from both sides. The only difference now was that from Delores, there was no hope there. There was no hope that she would be getting away any time soon. There was no hope at all.

"I'm s-sorry. Truly Pippa. Please let me go. Do Max, do him good and proper but please let me go."

It was Delores's last line of defence. A begging that she meant from the heart. From the soul. Pippa took in the warm breath of this woman and she tasted it. Then she hit her again, this time the other side of her face.

CHAPTER EIGHT

REWIND 6 – the past

There was a huge, huge explosion. One minute it had been pitch black. Like real pitch, pure black. Then all of a sudden the space was filled with this fire ball. Just before the fire ball a massive, massive white light that rendered everything in its most pure colour.

It was like a scene from one of those cataclysmic horror films. One of those with a spectacular ending. Against the fire that was raging after that bright white light, this girl was just in silhouette, but what a silhouette. One had the feeling that she wouldn't have provided such a mesmeric figure. It was the high heels that did that. In lots and lots of ways this girl was too young to be wearing high heels THIS high. But she wore them well. That was the thing. She wore them well. It was like she had worn heels like that for all of her young life. She looked so good in them because she was dressed, or more like shrink wrapped in a figure hugging micro length dress. The dress had to be rubber. It was one of those 'sexual dresses'. There was no other way that it could be described. A dress that looked like it had been made to small tolerances to fit her emerging figure.

She stood and she was holding something. Something that she had set off that chain of explosive events with. And now she was standing watching. Just watching the aftermath of what she had created. Of what she had caused in the place. That silhouette altered. Just changed stance a little bit. As though she was shifting her weight from one of her spiked heels to the other. There was other movement as well. Her hair. Yes it was her hair. Long, dead straight hair that swished across her rubbered back as she moved. One leg dead straight and splayed out a little. Her heels were separated on the floor. She was confident on those heels. Something about this silhouette told of her tender years. But also of

her confidence on those heels. Like as though she had been on them for some time. Like she hadn't just been experimenting with her mother's wardrobe items. But like these were her heels and she knew how to wear them. Her legs were long, tapered and they would develop the sexiest shape to them as she got older. And she knew how to walk in those heels. And now she was standing tall, watching what she had done.

It was like she could have just walked away. Could have just been that silhouette walking away, receding in size because her job had been done. And because there was no real reason why she needed to be there anymore. But there was more to it than this. The way she shifted her weight from heel to heel. There was more to it than she was idly watching. She was watching as though she had to make sure the job had been done properly. As though she couldn't leave there until she was sure that the job had been done. Like she had to make sure that whatever she had done couldn't be undone. That it had to stay done.

A few hours ago, this poor girl had been ruined and wrecked. Oh, her mind had been ruined and wrecked before this. But a few hours ago, physically she had been ruined and wrecked by the black man. He had slipped his cock into her back passage and he had ruined her that way. The hugeness of that cock was almost too much to comprehend. A huge cock that didn't take her age or her inexperience or her underdevelopment into consideration. A cock that was so thick, and yet again so slippery with her own produce and with so much baby oil that there was nothing to stop it doing what it did to her. Her parted her anus, stretched it wide. Then wider. Then wider and it travelled into the depths of her emerging femininity. She had thought she would die because of that pain. It was a terrible pain that she couldn't get over. That she would never get over. The type of pain that did things to a girl's mind. Things that stayed done. Things that couldn't be reversed. He had

ruined her back passage with that cock. Ruined it so that it couldn't be un-ruined. And he had flooded her with his semen. Totally ruined her. Fucked her up. Oh had she wished she was dead or what?

But he hadn't even been satisfied with that because he had then fucked her cunt – again. Once that monster cock had done her ass it did her cunt – again. That was painful but it was a different kind of pain. That was as much a pain in the mind, a psychological pain as it was a physical pain because of the fact that this man could help himself to her femininity. Just do as he pleased and with no recourse for his actions. The fact that her mother was there, watching, even instigating what was happening to her was another reason for that psychological pain. Fucking her deep. Unprotected full sex. Something that she would never get over. No matter how many times it happened to her. No matter how many times this man, and her mother abused her and misused her, she would never get over it. Him fucking her cunt like that, did things, different things to her mind. Even at her age she had had the thought, the questions, what if she got pregnant?

The icing on the cake though. Oh yes the icing on the cake. The genital mutilation that she had been subjected to by both this man and her mother. Actually, not by the man. On his instruction yes but by her mother. It had been her mother who had taken her sexuality away from her. Just taken it away with a scalpel and with some form of razor. That had hurt physically – not straight away though. That had been a gradual thing. A gradual increasing of the pain caused by those wounds that her mother had inflicted. There has been the 'cutting' sensation. She had felt that as she hung, but it didn't hurt as such. It had been just like there had been something taken away from her. Taken off her. Something no-one had any right to take off her. But her mother had done that. She had taken away the very essence of her own daughter's sexuality. The worst thing of all that could

happen to a young girl. And then the pain. That terrible pain that just got worse and worse. And the thing was that the pain seemed to simply blend and morph with the psychological pain that had been inflicted. A girl never got over being relieved of her clitoris function. Just liked she never got over being bitched by big dogs.

"Never feel sex again slut. You will just be a giver of pleasure and never have any yourself. How does that feel you little slut, hmm?"

His words hissing into her psyche. Those words hurting her. Hurting her deeply. She didn't understand sex and the sensations involved in sex but she understood that something had happened. Something big, something profound had happened to her when her mother had used that scalpel and that razor thing that she used. She understood that something big had taken place. It would be something that she would never be able to explain or describe but she felt 'incomplete' somehow. She felt as though part of her was missing. Not just physically but also mentally. That those little bits of flesh had been taken away and now she wasn't a proper girl any more. That she wasn't completely feminine any more. That day, as she hung suspended and as that most feminine piece of flesh had been taken from her, the clitoris hood, something else had been taken from her as well. Something that she would never completely or totally understand. But that man, that pervert man and her drug addled mother hadn't even been happy with that. They had then taken the tips, the very active tips off the nerve endings of her clitoris. She would never feel sex. Would never know orgasm. Would never know what real sex, loving sex, pure sex was all about. It was something that had been taken from her. Just taken away almost in a heartbeat.

If anything, that had been the thing that had played on her melting mind the most. The fact that she had had her femininity, the very core of her femininity taken away from her. Not just taken away, but taken away

cruelly. And then the knowledge that this man, this awful monster of a man was expecting her to provide pleasure to others. A pleasure that she would never be able to experience for herself. She didn't know about that pleasure, but somehow she knew that she would be missing out on a lot. Just the way this man hissed his words into her made it a profound thing that he was saying. That he was telling her. He was hissing at her like that because he wanted her to know what she would be mussing and what her future held in store for her – probably for the rest of her life.

It didn't help then that she had to suck this man clean after he had been inside both entrances to her femininity. That hadn't helped one little bit that she had been able to taste herself over that cock that was wedged into her mouth. It had felt like her jaws would dislocate because of the size of this man's black cock. What was it about that cock? It never seemed to get soft. Or go limp. A cock that was hard, solid hard all the time. And even after several spends inside her most intimate of orifices, he was still hard as she cleaned him. That made her retch. It made her retch to taste herself off this man's cock. It made her retch even more to feel her mother watching what she was doing. Oh yes she was off her face on the produce this man had provided her with in return for her 'services', but that didn't matter. She was still watching. She might have been semi focussing through a drug infested haze. But she was still watching. Watching what her little girl was doing. Somehow this girl had the hope that what her mother was seeing would damage her mother. She doubted though that it would damage her the way she herself had been damaged. Or to the extent she had been damaged. Cleaning that cock, tasting it. Wrapping her tongue round the bell end ridge – under it, scooping herself from under that ridge. Her taste. Her sexuality.

This was a girl who was learning about her merging womanhood in having it taken off her. Learning about it

in the most fucked up way. Learning about it in a back to front way. Learning it in the most damaging way. In a way it was the most complete and damaging mind fuck that could be inflicted on any individual – certainly on any girl. This was a girl who was having something else inflicted on her. A hatred. A hatred of her mother. A hatred of this man. This was a girl who was having her mind gripped and twisted in such a complete way that something had to give, something would give. At some point in the near future, in the very near future something would give in the most cataclysmic fashion.

But that wouldn't be yet. Not quite yet. First there would be the sexualisation of her. Or the continued sexualisation of her. She could have sex – correction she could never enjoy sex and yet she could give sexual pleasure to others. And so she would be sexualised. In the way she dressed. In the way she made up. All the things that she liked to do as a very young girl merging into young adulthood and beyond. All of that except that she would never be that complete and total woman because she had had that taken off her. Taken off her in the most obscene way. Sheer hose applied to her long legs. That should have been a sensual experience. Even an exciting one. Especially when the rubber dress had been pulled on and fitted to her. Wearing that rubber dress should have woken sexual urges and sexual exploration in her. She would never have known why that fabric or that texture was so sexy, or sexual. But it would be part of her emerging womanhood. It would be part of, the final part of her growing up. Instead there was nothing. She was turned into this sexual thing. This sexual doll but without the feelings and the sensations that should have gone with it. It was not an accident that this denial of her femininity worked to the negative on her mind. It was not an accident that this twisting of this young girl was being applied. It was a carefully crafted skill that was used to begin a process of ruining this young girl. A complete process. One that was both total

73

and irreversible. There would be no way back for this young girl. There would be no going back. Or no healing process. The damage being done to her would be so all encompassing, so total that there could only be a catastrophe waiting at some point in the future.

Slipping her feet into those ultra-high and spiked heels. They say high heels transform a woman's body and mind. Well that notion, that theory was blown apart with this poor young girl. Her sexuality was nil. It had been null and void and yet she still had this thing to deal with. This sexualisation. And the thing was that she was being sexualised in a sexual environment and so the effects were multiplied. It was like it was being rubbed in. Like she was having her nose rubbed in it. Like she was being tortured on multiple levels. First having her merging femininity take away in that brutal butchering way. And now being reminded of it by having to dress and make up in a sexual way. This should have been the time what her mom would be giving her hints and tips on makeup. But in this case the only words of wisdom her mother could come up with in her drug addled state were,

"The more of a slut you look the better he'll like it. I'm just telling you, that's all. For your own good."

It was like she knew what she was saying was wrong. All wrong. Like she was justifying, or trying, what she was saying. Like as though under all of that drug induced shit that she had going on, the mother in her was still there. That could have been looked on in a sympathetic light. Maybe. Except no. this situation, this horror was just too much for it to be brushed aside. Besides, the damage to the girl had been done. There was no going back. Already on that one way trip.

She might have known what her mother was saying was all wrong but she also knew what she meant. She also knew what she had to look like. She knew what it meant to look like a slut. A rubber dressed slut. All legs and lipstick and with so much mascara on that it

74

practically dripped from her eyelashes. Her dressing and making up the way 'required' was like an additional strain on an already fucked up mind. And as the future. Or her likely future dawned on her more and more, it was like something too much for her to comprehend. Her life ahead. How she would have to live. How she would have to exist. Thinking about sexually gratifying others – maybe even people more perverted than this black man, was too much for her head to cope with. Something had to give. Standing in front of a full length mirror, rubbered up, hosed up, heeled up to the max, lipsticked up she was seeing herself for what she was. A sexual freak. She could look normal she guessed. But she would never feel normal and that was the thing. She would never 'feel' normal. And she would always be fucked up in the head. In the mind.

This poor fucked up girl had been given time to make herself look good for the black man. For the black man who had ruined her life. That might have been his one and only mistake in what otherwise had been a flawless plan. Flawless in planning and in execution. He would spend some time watching mummy get high, and then higher still. A little game in his own head. Make sure the girl knew what she had to look like, provide everything she would need to do just that and then leave her to it. Wait for the reveal as it were. His one and only mistake. Not getting mummy to watch her. Not getting mummy to be with her all the time. Giving her time to do her own thing. Taking for granted that she would do what he wanted her to do. What he needed her to do. Assuming that what she had been through already had been enough to have broken her completely and that she would simply do what he wanted. That she had simply rolled over. A lot might understand that if she had rolled over. All that she had been through. And knowing what the future held for her. Or at least having a hint dropped onto her about what the future held for her. It would be understandable if she had rolled over and broken

completely.

The thing was that she hadn't. Something inside her had clicked into place. Maybe something of the survivor that all human beings have buried inside them. But something else had clicked into place and had emerged as well. Something murderous. She had been given time alone. A lot of time alone. The black man and her mother basking in what they had achieved in their own imitable ways. Whilst they thought it was all good in the hood, the girl was preparing the fire bomb. The fire bomb that would be preceded by a stun explosion. The bright white flash followed by the all-consuming fireball. Where she got the 'ingredients' or the knowledge to do what she did would remain a mystery forever. Maybe it was just the desperate survivalist. Maybe it was the buried, murderous intent that was in her all the time. Maybe she was the sum of the parts that she was. Or the result of what had been done to her over the years. Who knows?

She had done the reveal. She had shown the man what he wanted to see. Her slutted up. Maxed out. A sexual doll with no sexuality of her own. And he had revelled in that image. In that vision. And then she had let go of the pressure sensitive switch she had been holding. The bright, bright white light had stunned the man and the girl's mother. She had rigged that room up. Had taken the time to rig it up so that there would be no escape. Then there was the fireball. There has been no screams, no crying from the man or her mother. Shock would have taken care of that. It would have rendered them silent enough for the fire to consume them. No sound at all. The stun blast had done its job. So had the fireball. The place would burn to the ground. And it did. And she turned and walked away. At last she could do that – walk away. She had got her freedom back. But to whose cost? Pippa was free but guess who was paying the real cost, right now.

CHAPTER NINE

Now

Pippa had begun the finishing touches to Delores. That is, she had begun the end game. But she was alternating between Max and Delores. She wanted the both of them to reach the end game together. She wanted them each to know what was in store for the other. It was an added torture for them. An added layer of despair. Knowing what the other was in for. Knowing what was going to happen to them. It was a case of the knowing what the other was going through would be worse than the torture they themselves would go through. The body would begin to shut down. The shock and the fear would do that. To an extent they would be numb to their own pain. But not to the pain of the other. It was no accident that Pippa worked it like that. That she applied that extra final layer of distress and despair into the mix. It was no accident that she worked towards an end game either. For her there always had to be an 'end game'. It was just the way it was with her. The way she was made up. The way it had to be. The way it always was. She never let it be thought that an ordeal would end any time soon. She might leave little holes of hope that she would cruelly seal up. But on the whole she would never let her victims thinks that the ordeal was going to end. She certainly never let them think there would be an end game of sorts. That was the thing about Pippa – she didn't let any anything out unless she wanted to. If she let anything out, then it was because she wanted to. Or because she needed to as part of the end game.

"I'm feeding this down your throat Delores. All you have to do is 'swallow' as I push."

It was another of her 'kinks'. To get her victims to help in their own demise. To get them to assist in their own end game without really knowing it was their endgame. She was pushing something – a latex

something into Delores's mouth. A tube, or something. A long tube. Windpipe sized tube. Delores didn't like it. She didn't like it at all and it scared her. It scared her a lot as she began to swallow. That tube was smooth and it seemed to slide down her through with ease. She could feel it sliding down. And she didn't need to consciously swallow as she had been told. Rather her throat went into an automatic swallowing action. But the thing was the deeper it went, the more her breathing was affected. She could still breath but it was different. It felt different. It felt more laboured. Harder for her to breath. She whimpered, she couldn't help whimpering. Pippa knew that she wouldn't be able to stop herself whimpering and she didn't expect it. It was part of her joy as a sadist. To hear that fear coming out, to see and hear it manifest itself in various ways. With Delores, it was that whimper. A nice wet, slippery whimper.

"That's a good, good girl. Just swallow. Let it take the breathing off you Delores. Let it do it for you."

Delores couldn't work out what she was being told to do by this maniac. Her mind wouldn't work properly. Couldn't work properly. Then it hit her. As she swallowed the tube, that smooth latex tube was taking the place of her windpipe and she was being forced to breathe through that. She could feel her throat, or her windpipe filled with this latex. She could feel the sides of her windpipe being forced out and out. It didn't feel right. It was harder for her to breath but at the same time it was uncomfortable bordering on painful. Delores was in such a state by this time that she didn't think, didn't even know how far in the tube would be fed. The thought of where the other end of that tube went didn't cross her mind. She certainly could see, as she swallowed, the strapping and the harness which was part of the tube coming up closer and closer to her head, and face and mouth.

There was like a silence. A silence that seemed to

go on forever. There were two police officers. A uniformed male and a plain clothes detective woman. Eventually, Grace spoke slowly like she was trying to get something through to someone of limited intelligence. People in her circle usually did that. It somehow made them feel better about themselves. Fed the superiority complex that they already had.

"I'm tell you there is something wrong. These people don't just vanish. You need to look into it as a matter of urgency. I have a bad, bad feeling about this. A real bad feeling."

She gave the impression she had been trying to get her point across for some time and that she was getting impatient. The two officers looked, and quite frankly acted the way they looked. Bored. The woman detective spoke and she mimicked this woman's patronising tone.

"I'm sorry, but this Max and Delores are two grown up people. Successful people right? Ok, they've gone somewhere and not told anyone about where they have gone. Maybe they wanted it that way. Maybe they didn't want their so called friends to know they were planning a weekend, or a week away from home. Did you think that maybe they wanted it that way? There have been no reports of accidents. There are no sign, or no evidence that anything untoward had happened. From where I am sitting, there is nothing for me to investigate. In fact I cannot allocate resources to this, at the moment. I tell you what, I don't think there is anything wrong and I think this Delores and Max will surface eventually. But, if you leave it another 48 hours, and still nothing – if this couple haven't shown for work – and I find it hard to believe that given their occupations, that they won't show up for work, then I will take a closer look personally. How does that sound? At least after 48 hours I will have something tangible to go on and we can swing things into motion from this end."

There was another one of those silences. Grace was pretty much in despair which was an unusual thing for

her. She had rested her forehead in the palm of her hand, and then she snapped into the upright position in her chair.

"Ok, ok. Have your 48 hours. But I am telling you there is something wrong here. Very wrong. 48 hours could be too long. But have it your way. It comes down on your head if this ends badly. That's all I'm saying."

Grace got up to leave and the woman detective looked across at her colleague. There was an exchange of looks. Probably both thought that Grace had some sort of reason to be worried. But in missing person cases their hands were tied. Essentially, in this case, Max and Delores were not missing people. They were adult human beings who could well have decided to jet off without telling anyone. Certainly their lifestyles would suggest that could have been the case. If they had been children who had vanished without trace the things would be different. And if anyone knew that this couple were in the hands of a lunatic that had all but escaped from the asylum – then all the stops would be pulled out to find them.

"I will be in touch I can assure you."

Grace was not happy as she left. She had done all she could. She had even been round to the house in the burbs. The house that Max and Delores owned together. There had been nothing. It was in darkness. She had even waited outside, in her car, hoping to see them coming back. Or some sign of life in the house at all. Nothing. It had been after that stake out that she had decided to get in touch with the local police. And as it happened, that had come to nothing as well. At least, for 48 hours it wouldn't come to anything. But by the time those hours had elapsed, it could well be too late.

Delores's head was fully harnessed. A web of shiny black rubber strapping held her head tight. And her mouth was sealed. If truth be known, she looked akin to an alien. Sitting there, all harnessed up. And where her

mouth should have been was more rubber. Like a rubber blanking plate behind which her stretched lips and open mouth existed. Like she had been silenced in some horrific way. An alien who would be later interrogated by the authorities. There were other rubber tubes as well as the one coming from the mouth section of that harness. One snaking from between Delores's open legs and one coming from under her ass cheeks. That third tube made her sit awkward on the chair. But she had had to be sitting on that chair because swallowing that tube all the way, and then having those other tubes pushed into the depths of her intimate femininity was only the beginning of a deeper ordeal for her. She had been through enough – the blank staring of her eyes was enough to say that. She had never been more frightened, or more petrified in her life. And now it was like the fear and the petrification had worn her down. Not desensitised her to it, but just made her accept that the future for her was not a good one. She had sat there for a long time wondering, silently fearful of what the next step for herself would be.

Max had seen it all. Part of the game. Him knowing what was in store for his partner. Not knowing, but at least guessing that it was not going to be a good thing. He had his own things to deal with. His cock had been corkscrewed open by Pippa. She had loved doing that. Twisting that sound deeper and deeper. Each twist bringing a screeching kind of wounded animal sound that grated on the nerves of anyone who heard it. Delores heard it. And she witnessed it but she had her shit going on as well. Pippa had enjoyed so much making Max suffer. She hated men. Her past dictated that she would always hate men. Or hate the male of the species. But then she didn't like other women or girls much either. Come to think of it, she didn't like other people period. She preferred her own company unless she was making others that might have been in her company suffer in some inhumane way. She glanced over at Delores as she

spoke to Max.

"Time to pay the piper isn't it Max my boy? Time to make you REALLY suffer."

She spoke as though she had spent the last two days tickling and play fighting with the man who was seriously afraid for his own life right now. She had left his cock corkscrewed that way to work on Delores but now she was back. She had screwed that sound all the way in. He didn't know, or couldn't know how deeply the sound was embedded. If he had had any idea then he would have known that the end of the sound was inside her bladder and was hanging there. Cruelly Pippa had let the weight of that sound add to the absolute pain he was in. She had taken the twist handle off the sound and replaced it with a screw in extension hose. Another rubber hose but this time a smaller gage higher pressure type hose. All of those rubber hoses snaked and vanished into the floor of the basement. Inside that hose was an airline, but also a separate electric wire compartment.

Pippa had to give it to this couple. They had fully equipped this place for their little hobbies but would never have even the slightest clue about how to use most of the stuff they had bought. She reasoned with herself that probably Delores was the one with delusions of grandeur. She had been the one probably who had consulted with all manner of people from the fetish and torture scenes about what she should buy and what she should have fitted into that room. Pippa smiled wryly to herself. It was ironic that Delores was now in this end game. It was such a delicious irony that Pippa couldn't help but smile to herself like that. Pippa knew about that stuff in that room. She knew all about it. Since her childhood, pain had been the name of her game in various guises. Taking it and inflicting it. She knew how to use all of that stuff. And if she didn't know, then she soon worked it out. It was like she was in a playground of her own design.

It wasn't like Pippa didn't know what the effects of

turning that compressed air tap on the micro hose to the cock sound would be. She knew that there would be another barrage of utter wailing sound the moment that she turned it. And there was. There was the hiss – like a concentrated hiss of compressed air that came from 'somewhere'. That corkscrew spiralling down inside the cock core immediately expanded creating the type of pain that didn't belong in the real world. Inside that still erect cock, the sound was forcing the tube walls out. That constriction, that pressure creating that pain. Inside his bladder, from the end of the sound, a little bubble or balloon of rubber sprouted and began to inflate. It was a micro controlled thing. The corkscrew inflating and the bladder balloon inflating in unison and in a micro controlled way. That bladder balloon causing immediate increase in pressure. That balloon taking the place of the collected urine. That urine forced to displace somewhere. Where? Against the bladder walls. There was no way or means that Max could release the contents of his bladder. That was now controlled. Not just controlled, but that urine being used to create more and more torture. Pippa set something, a little dial on the tape that she had turned. Set it to a pre-setting and then stood back and watched the magic work. And for her it did work. This was a man at the end of his tether. Pippa reckoned quite rightly that this man would be wishing he was dead right now. She reckoned that right at this time, as that inserted sound and balloon were doing their work, that this man was wishing that someone would come along with a gun, blow his head off. Put him out of his misery. Not yet though. It wasn't time for that yet. Pippa knew also that Max wouldn't have a clue if or when his ordeal would end. She moved into Max as the cycle of inflation ran its course. She marvelled at how twisted and contorted his face was. And those sounds. Oh those noises that he made. Way beyond the usual screams of agony that were always the first step. The noises that he made came from somewhere else. They

came come somewhere that could not be guessed at. Or from somewhere that was inaccessible to other human beings. Where those noises he was making were coming from was a special place. Pippa knew about that special place. She knew about it because she had been there herself. She had been there. Had existed there. And now she had the key to that place so that she could take others there. Max was there already. He was in that place. And now she wanted to take Delores there as well. She wanted this couple to be reunited. But reunited in her own way. In her special way and in her special place. That special place.

Delores had watched her man taken to that place. It would be an understatement to say that she didn't like what she was seeing. That what she was seeing made her flesh creep. But then she wouldn't have known that she was seeing it and feeling those effects because she was supposed to. That it was all part of the game. Part of the end game as it were. When it was her turn to be taken to that place her mind was still affected, still infested with the sight and sounds of Max suffering. Arguably the worst had been saved for Delores. Arguably Pippa hated women more than she hated men, although in this setting that difference was arbitrary. She moved in to Delores and Delores visibly shuddered. Her throat, filled with that rubber tube constantly rolled in a swallowing motion. It was a natural reaction to having an alien object down inside her windpipe. Then there was the hiss of compressed air again. The pre-setting being flicked and the stockinged and heeled Pippa standing back and waiting for the delay to pass and then the hiss of compressed air. Delores's eyes bulging open. Wide open. The tube in her throat expanding out. Widening the tube and stretching her windpipe in the process. That expansion affecting the whole length of the tube. And from the ends of the tube in her windpipe, other smaller tubes appearing to grow and snake into her lungs. That tube taking over her breathing entirely. Pippa watched

84

and at first there was no smile. But then the smile came. Just about the time when their eyes made contact with each other. There was this smile. Not a cruel smiling. Just knowing one. Pippa knew what this woman was going through. What she was feeling and how frightened she was. She shouldn't have known that, but she did. Pippa nibbled her lip at the sight of Delores's bulging windpipe. It looked like it was swollen. It looked like an alien was going down inside her.

That was the thing, Pippa knew. She knew everything. She knew because she had been there. She moved her fingers to the dial and pre-setting on the vaginal tube. And at the same time she did the anal one. Behind the pseudo-gag there were noises. No doubt they were noises of utter distress and pain. Her throat would have been in dire pain. And she would still be getting used to having her breathing controlled and regulated.

"Try to relax Delores. If you stress too much then it will be harder for you to breath. This system takes your stress into consideration. I'm not saying it will be easy for you to relax, it won't. But it you don't relax it will be harder for you to breath. The more stressed you become the harder it will be. If you get too stressed, your breathing will be cut altogether. So you have to try to relax. Relax and absorb. You're going to suffer but you need to just try to make that easier for yourself rather than harder."

Pippa spoke with something like a restrained glee in her voice. The two tubes hissed to life at the same time. And the expansion in Delores's vaginal and anal tunnels happened at exactly the same time. The stretching, the filling and the extra tubes sprouting from the ends to find all those nooks and crannies. The vaginal tubes finding her womb, her bladder – all of her reproductive organs and bits and pieces. And once they had found those bits and pieces, stretching them, hurting them. Controlling them. The anal tube stretching her beyond the normal parameters. Pippa had early on worked out that this

equipment had had the safety devices removed. Safety devices that would not allow the tubes to be expanded beyond safe levels. She had smiled to herself again at that. This couple were something she had to admit. She stood back and watched Delores in all her agony. And there was agony. Pure undiluted agony. It was written all over her face. But there was more than that. More than agony there. There was undiluted fear as well. Fear for the future. Fear for her future. Max and Delores experiencing each other's torture in their own basement play room. Soundproofed playroom. No sound out. No sound in.

CHAPTER TEN

Funny how things work out. How what goes around comes around and all that. Pippa was still bathing in the afterglow of what she had done. It was an afterglow and yet it wasn't over yet. It was just that another passage had passed. Another point in time had been reached. Delores and Max would no longer be in any doubt as to their future. Or rather they would no longer be harbouring any thought that there would be a way out of this for them. That they would get out to live another day. That they might not live any more days in fact. Pippa knew all of this. She knew the kind of things that would be going through this couple's minds. She knew that their minds would be in overdrive. It didn't matter about the pain, and there was a LOT of that, that they were going through. The minds would be racing. Trying and failing to make sense of it all. And there would be regret. Oh would there be lots of regret. It didn't matter if every one of their nerve endings was in shreds, and they were, they would be trying to work it all out. And they would be feeling very, very sorry for themselves. But Pippa liked it at this stage of what she did. She liked it when the chips were right down for the couple. She liked it when there was nothing more, for the time being that she had to do. She liked it when she could bath in this after glow.

It was always at this point, at the point that there was nothing else to do for the time being that she could stroke herself at last. Even though her clitoris hood and her clitoris tip had been removed when she was very, very young by her mother and that black man, she still had the desire there. There was still that 'desire' there. The sexual desire. Pippa didn't know much about sexual gratification, or mutual sexual gratification. She had had that part of her life, the learning, the flowering, and the blossoming into womanhood taken away from her. And so all she had left was the 'desire'. That desire like the

knowledge that there was something she was missing. And so the desire, that sexual desire was something for her. Something that was nothing to do with anyone else. Something. As she got older she knew that she was missing orgasms. And where orgasms remained a mystery to most people, for some reason she resented the fact that she would never be able to explore orgasms, and the various ways to enjoy them and create them. All she was left with was the desire. The desire never went. And that was the thing – the desire never abated. If Pippa had been able to orgasm then perhaps she would have escaped her own vicious circle. But she never could orgasm. That ability was gone. So all she had was the constant desire. And it was that. It was a constant desire. It could have well been a fact that it wasn't what she had suffered all those years ago was the factor in how her life of carnage was to evolve at all. It could have, more than likely was the fact that she could not complete the sex act. There was no orgasm, no gratification, no afterglow of sex. All she had was the desire. A constant desire. The desire was still there when she basked in the afterglow of what she had done to people. After what she had done to Max and Delores. But this was her reflective time. This was her time to 'rest' if rest was the word. No orgasm, no recovery after intense sex. Just reflective time. Quiet time. And that stroking of her slit. The slit that was always wet and slippery. That never went away either. The desire never went and that wetness never went either. All there was, was orgasm denial.

Quiet time – there was a joke in their somewhere. It was anything but quiet in that basement. There had been a degree of torture applied to both Delores and Max that would defy belief. Certainly if the scene was stumbled upon by some innocent it would be feasible that it would remain imprinted on their minds for years to come. No-one would get over that sight. Or that scene. Or those sounds that came from the captive couple. Captive couple made it sound almost as though they were wholly

innocent in this. They weren't. And yet, one would come to the conclusion that no-one living deserved to suffer like this. No one.

Pippa wasn't a smoker. She didn't have a habit. But she did occasionally enjoy a cigarette. She had been known to do so socially. And she always enjoyed one during this reflective phase of the absolute carnage that she caused. The sounds had changed. There was no out and out screaming any more, not like when she had skinned Max's cock and sliced the ball sack open so that the testicles could just hang through the wound on their own tubes and entrails. He had screamed when she had done that. Oh had he screamed. If he had just, if he had JUST shut the fuck up, he would have realised that there was little if any pain involved in what she was doing at that precise time. The scalpel that Pippa used was so sharp, so clinically sharp that pain just did not happen. It was simply what the mind did to a person. All he would feel would be the 'tug' of those tubes with the weight of his testicles. His mind did the rest and that resulted in his screaming with utter terror.

Pippa had rolled a huge mirror in front of Max before she had started doing the unthinkable so that this man could watch in full what she was doing. It was what he saw that made him scream not what he felt. A slice down the underside, down the seam of the cock, and then around under the ridge of the bell end so that the foreskin fell away. And then more careful, precision scalpel work to remove the shaft skin around the top of the balls. Peeling it away, discarding it like it was just garbage. All the time that corkscrew sound inside him and that balloon filling his bladder forcing his urine to displace. The sound tube stretching his own inside tubes against their own elasticity. Oh there was pain. A constant pain but Pippa was of the thought that this man shouldn't be such a wimp. After all he raped and abused women. What right did he have to be such a wimp? A cock and ball scalping was the least he deserved.

A skinned cock was a weird sight. Pippa had meted out this kind of thing before to those who she felt deserved it and she never quite got over the sight of an erect, skinned cock. More so with Max and this sound thing inside it. There would have been an agony inside and out. Once those scalpel wounds had sent the messages to an already fucked up brain there would be the wall of sound noise of a level not reached before by this man. Probably at the precise point of realisation that his life would end very soon. That this was indeed the end game. At the point that he would have gladly taken a bullet to the head. But that would have been too quick. Too easy. It would have been a way out and if there was anything more certain than Pippa not giving ways out to her victims, it would have been crystal clear. Pippa had withstood that wall of sound, those inhumane screams from Max. In a way she had bathed in them as well. She enjoyed her victim's despair and yet in her mind she would have been telling this man not to be such a wimp. She would have liked that noise but not for too long. The novelty would have worn off and when it did, at that point that the noise became something other than a wall of sound she would have had that cigarette. And as this stockinged and heeled psychopath dragged, inhaled and exhaled through red lips she would have smiled – just a little smile at the thought of the renewed wall of sound, and even louder, nerve shredding wall of sound and she cut his balls loose. Rubbing herself and smoking at the same time. It was what Pippa lived for. What she had lived for, for a long time. This was her release. Where there was no orgasm, there was this. And it was this she lived for.

The first time Pippa had smiled wide for a long time was when she cut the balls of this man loose. Cutting them loose may have been over egging it a bit. She simply inserted the scalpel into the sack seam and then drew it up and around until the sack opened. Then she peeled it back until the two balls popped out. Hanging by

his reproductive plumbing. Even Pippa would have to admit that when Max saw that scene looking back at him from the mirror, she thought that his heart might give out there and then. It didn't. Instead that wall of sound. That wall of sound that slowly died to a whimper. But it was more than a whimper. There was something melancholy about it. A melancholy whimper.

"You know don't you Max? You know it's all over for you? But not just yet."

Pippa had dragged and inhaled, and then lazily blew out smoke. Subconsciously she had taken her stroking finger up and she had held it under her flared nostrils smelling herself. She was gloating, in a way.

There had been a lot of noise from Delores as well. But that had been a different kind of noise. Pippa always treated her women victims differently. Maybe because there was that feminine connection. Maybe because there were those strings, no matter how fine those strings were, of sympathy for them. Maybe Pippa would admit that she wished she didn't have to do to women and girls what she did. But that other person inside would always win out there. That psychopath inside her would always win out. She might be left with those strings of sympathy – the fine threads that let this sadist exist and function in the normal world. But her sadism would win out.

There had been no doubt that with those final bursts of compressed air into the inserts that she had slipped into Delores, she caused massive internal trauma. That was damage that was not just skin deep, but femininity deep. That was one woman ruining another woman in a physical way and yet in a mental way as well. The physical scars, the physical flesh may have healed, had it been allowed to, eventually. But the scars on the mind would remain. Those inserts stretching Delores's anal tunnel and her vaginal plumbing until she bled inside. And yet as that wholly different wall of sound noise engulfed the basement, so Pippa stroked Delores. She stroked her where her clitoris hood was. And she stroked

her in such a way that her clitoris filled and swelled and then popped out of the hood. And there it was for Pippa to see. She had been denied her own clitoris. That had been taken from her by her mother and that monster black man – her mother's dealer. But now she had this clitoris to play with. And oh did she play with it.

"One last orgasm Delores?"

What was she talking about – this nut job? One last orgasm. It was doubtful that the older woman would be thinking in terms of orgasm. Now with what she had seen happen to Max. and not with the predicament that she herself was in. it would have become clear to Delores now as well that her time on this world was about to come to an end. Or about to end soon. The last thing she would be thinking about would be an orgasm. And yet the way Pippa could focus the minds of others, especially her victims was a trick, like magic that she had learned. The thought that this woman, this chameleon like woman could force an orgasm onto a woman who was coming to terms with the end of her life was almost too much for the senses to get a grip of. That thought. Orgasm at a time like this. And yet as Pippa played with that clitoris. As she pressed and rubbed it and manipulated it, Delores began to respond. It would have been a further torture for her to respond like that but there was no doubt about it, her body was betraying her. It was betraying her big style as Pippa's fingers swirled and pressed. And as she enforced that production of slippery oily fluid.

"That's a good girl. Good girl. I know you're gonna hate me for this Delores but you know. I like to give one last little treat before... well, you know, before."

She left the sentence unfinished. Left it hanging in the air as she rubbed and pressed. And as she got down closer to the clitoris she blew over it. Made it swell more and more. Made it look purple and as though it was a grape that was about to drop from the bush. Except there was no bush. Just the smooth hairlessness of Delores's

sexuality. Pippa blowing and blowing and rubbing at the same time. Not rubbing the entire slit. Just rubbing those eight thousand nerve endings that made up the clitoris. Focussing the 'pleasure' on that area. Making the orgasm that was building, clitoris based as opposed to bodily based. Focussing it in that one small area of the clit tip. Using her finger tips and her nails in that way. Forcing the unreleased pleasure to mount up and collect behind that clitoris tip and keeping it there. Just keeping it there until she, that is Pippa was ready to let it out. Delores becoming aroused in her mind as well as her clitoris. In a way this was the cruellest of the cruel. Delores had come to terms with the fact that her life would in all probability be ending any time soon. Any time soon. And yet this other woman, this mad woman was now taking her to another place. She was taking her to that sexual place. It was place she shouldn't have been allowed anywhere near at this point in her ending life. And yet she was. She had been taken there and now she was being allowed to wallow in that pleasure. But even that was a torture for her. It was a torture for her because of the fact that Pippa was encouraging the orgasm to build and build behind that clit tip but she wasn't allowing a release, not yet. She was controlling Delores's sexuality like she was controlling and torturing everything else. She would build and build that orgasm to such a point that Delores would crave its release. She would need that release but even then she wouldn't let it go. Not straight away.

But that release. Oh that release when it came was one to savour. It was one to wallow in for Delores but it was one to savour for Pippa. An intense hit of absolute pleasure. That amount of pleasure in amongst that amount of despair and agony didn't seem right. It made the world as a whole seem a fucked up place. But that orgasm would have been the best orgasm that Delores would ever have experienced. Ironic that it was in the passage that would be leading up to her death at the

hands of this female sadist. Delores wouldn't have even noticed, not at first, at the height of that orgasm, Pippa wielding the scalpel again and then 'slicing' the clitoris off. Not just the tip of the clitoris. The whole lot so it was flush with the rest of her flesh. A clitoris no more. Nothing. The hood gone. The clit gone. And then the wall of sound again. Pure pleasure followed by pure agony both physical and psychological. The orgasm gone.

Pippa was wearing that clitoris in a little phial around her neck as she smoked that cigarette. The clit was floating around in some sort of solution just like the black man had worn her clitoris hood in a phial and solution. The wall of noises now down to those inhumane whimperings. Whimperings of human beings knowing that they were going to have their lives ended for them by this woman.

Pippa was in such a world of her own that she didn't sense there being something wrong. In a way she was dropping the ball. Noises in the basement would have drowned out any noises from above. Not that there were many noises from above. Disturbances maybe. The very slight noise of a lock being forced. A window being broken. Nothing that would have filtered down. Nothing at all. Even the door to the basement was opened carefully, quietly. No noise of steps. Pippa wallowing in that aftermath. She didn't even see the dancing red dots over her own torso. She didn't have a clue she was in the sights of Special Forces until it too late. She had dragged and inhaled on that cigarette and she had sat back, her eyes closed. She had been thinking of the final end game. How she would finish off Delores and Max. She had been thinking that it would have to be spectacular. It would have to surpass anything she had done before. She had smiled to herself, her eyes still closed. The beginning of a death plan for the couple coming together in her mind. Ah she would enjoy this one. She was going to reap all she could from this one. This was her best yet.

There was no reason why she opened her eyes when she did. But they snapped open. Those huge, gorgeous eyes just snapped open and there were all these people. And all these guns pointed at her. It was all over for her. One might have expected her to have made a sudden move, so that she would be shot dead on the spot. There had obviously been special attention paid to her – Special Forces on her case and all that. But she didn't make that sudden move. She didn't move at all. There was a survivor in Pippa. One that not many would get or understand. A deep down survivor. It was all over for her. For now.

There were blues and twos everywhere. The outside of the property seemed bathed in the light of police vehicles. And medical services. It seemed like nothing happened for a long time. Lots of uniformed and non-uniformed people hanging round doing nothing. Nothing visible at least. It was only very gradually that word got around. It was happening. The lunatic was being taken out and away. And then she was. Helicopters hovered above. Press and TV were not allowed onto the same road. They had been kept away. There would be largely radio silence on this until the authorities knew what they were dealing with. Pippa was taken out, cuffed, expressionless. Officers that had been inside that house obviously disturbed by what they had seen down in that basement huddled together in groups. Some talking. Some not saying anything at all. It all went silent, even the choppers overhead seemed to go silent as Pippa was taken out, and away. As she had been loaded into the back of an unmarked car she had looked up and immediately she had eye contact with a woman. That woman was Grace. That eye contact seemed to last an age. Just pure, pure eye contact. A shudder went down the spine of Grace. She would never know where that shudder came from or why. Pippa had been making mental notes at that time. A photographic memory imprinting Grace's image on her mind for later

consumption. She knew – Pippa knew that somehow this woman was responsible for her capture. She would deal with that, in due course. Another victim for her in the future. Already she liked the look of Grace. She was another one of 'those' type of women that she liked to work on. There was just the hint of a smile from Pippa as that eye contact was broken in the chaos, and as she was taken away.

Those choppers overhead were even more silent as the couple, the victims, Delores and Max were taken out. They were alive. The authorities had got to them before it was too late. Both on wheeled stretchers. Both with fluid lines into them. It would take the authorities an age to unravel what had happened here. Even then they might not get all the answers.

THE END

9 781786 950086